Cock<u>tales</u>

First Edition

Published by The Nazca Plains Corporation
Las Vegas, Nevada
2009

ISBN: 978-1-935509-16-5

Published by

The Nazca Plains Corporation ®
4640 Paradise Rd, Suite 141
Las Vegas NV 89109-8000

PUBLISHER'S NOTE
Cocktales is a work of fiction created wholly by *Lew Bull*'s imagination. All characters are fictional and any resemblance to any persons living or deceased is purely by accident. No portion of this book reflects any real person or events.

Cover Cocktail, Tracy Hebden
Art Director, Blake Stephens

DEDICATION

To Mark and Nicholas, OD, Daisy and Joseph
- one big happy family.

- INTRODUCTION -

This is a book with a difference. The idea behind it was to create a series of erotic short stories to accompany a collection of equally erotic cocktails to be enjoyed while reading the book. Preceding each story is the recipe for an exotic cocktail to fit the accompanying story.

Enjoy the fun of mixing these cocktails and at the same time enjoy the pleasure of reading the stories.

Lew Bull

Cock*tales*

First Edition

Lew Bull

TABLE OF CONTENTS

- COCKTAIL RECIPES -

- STORIES -

- SINGAPORE SLING -

Ingredients:

1 dash Cherry Liqueur
4 oz Club Soda
1 oz Gin
½ oz Grenadine
2 oz bottled Sour mix
Cracked ice
Cubes ice

Directions:

Fill a mixing glass with ice. Add gin, sour mix, and Grenadine. Shake and strain into a Collins glass filled with ice cubes. Fill with Club Soda and top with cherry brandy.

SINGAPORE SLING

The early evening traffic of people and vehicles made their way down the tree and shopping mall-lined Orchard Road, all heading home after another busy, hot and humid Singaporean day. Gregory Fook, a local businessman, chose instead to travel by air-conditioned cab to the world renowned Raffles Hotel to have a sundowner before heading home.

The Raffles Hotel stood majestically in its entire colonial splendor as the last rays of the sun caught its gleaming white facade. Gregory alighted from the cab, entered the hotel and made his way to the Palm Garden to view his favorite object, the ornate cast-iron fountain dating back to the 1890s which, surrounded by tall palm trees, was to him a tranquil haven of peace. The tinkling of the spraying fountain water acted as a relaxant from the hustle and bustle of the city outside. Gregory spent some time here in the garden's quiet surrounds while his mind, after a busy business day, unwound. When he felt he had relaxed sufficiently, he ventured into the main hotel and headed to a bar for a drink. He sat down at the bar counter and ordered from the young barman.

"Good evening, sir. Nice to see you again. It's been a few days since we last saw you," said the amiable young barman. "Your usual, sir?"

Gregory nodded and the barman began getting Gregory's drink for him. The barman brought the drink, placed it on the counter in front of Gregory and smiled.

"One Singapore Sling, sir."

Gregory, returned the smile, paid and lifted the glass to his lips. It was refreshing.

"How long have you been working here, Michael?" enquired Gregory of the barman.

"Just coming up for two years, sir," he replied, his eyes alight and his smile beaming. "And how long have you been coming in here for a drink, sir?"

"Oh probably three or four years I suppose," replied Gregory.

"And it's always the same drink," laughed Michael, busying himself behind the bar as he spoke.

Gregory raised his glass, almost as a toast to Michael and laughed as well. A few more customers entered the bar so Michael headed in their direction to serve them, but throughout this, Gregory found himself watching Michael all the time. When his glass was empty, he called Michael and ordered another drink.

"Would you like a drink?" Gregory asked Michael.

"Not while I'm on duty, thanks sir, but I am going off duty in another half an hour's time. Also we're not allowed to drink on the premises, so we would have to go somewhere else if you wanted to have a drink with me, sir."

"No problem," said Gregory. "When you get off duty, you just say where and we can go to have a drink."

Michael continued with his duties for the next half an hour until his shift was completed and then he informed Gregory; "Meet me in the Palm Garden and we can go from there," said Michael, leaning across the bar counter and almost whispering to Gregory.

When they both reached the Palm Garden, Gregory turned to Michael and said, "I would like to take you for a drink, but I would also like to spend some time with you, Michael."

Michael smiled at Gregory, wondering what was going through Gregory's head, but then he couldn't just assume that Gregory might have ulterior motives.

Gregory looked like a very ordinary thirty-something man who probably had a wife and family and led a very ordinary life. Michael, on the other hand was a twenty-three year old man, in the exciting times of his life who wanted fun. Sure, Gregory was interesting to talk to in a bar situation, but what did this man mean by 'I would like to spend some time with you'?

"What did you have in mind?" asked Michael when they emerged from the hotel and stood outside in the street.

"I thought we might go somewhere where we could have a drink together and maybe be private, if you know what I mean," replied Gregory.

Michael thought for a moment and then said, "I know just the place, if I understand you properly. I'll take you there and you can see if that's what you had in mind."

They hailed a cab and set off for Telok Ayer Street where Michael knew of a club where they could have a drink and other things, so to speak, and if this wasn't the place for Gregory, at least Michael could stay and spend some time there having fun.

"Where are we going?" Asked Gregory.

"A place I know of where you can have a drink and still be together and private. If it's not what you like, we can go somewhere else," continued Michael.

The cab eventually arrived at the given address and Michael paid and they made their way to the club's entrance.

"What is this place?" enquired Gregory, looking up at the neon-lighted sign above the entrance.

"It's a men's club," answered Michael.

Gregory's face never gave his thoughts away, but his mind raced on hearing this. He didn't know what to expect if he entered and he now wasn't quite sure if he was doing the right thing. Michael smiled at him as if to say 'you'll be fine', paid and led Gregory inside.

Michael took Gregory into a change room where he told Gregory they could get undressed. At first Gregory was startled by the idea, but soon realized that everyone that he saw was naked. After disrobing, Michael then led him to the bar where they sat down and ordered drinks together. Soon Gregory began to relax at the realization that they were not the only naked men in the venue.

"What is this place?" whispered Gregory to Michael.

"It's a place where men can come together, if you'll excuse the pun," laughed Michael, "and be themselves, away from prying eyes."

Gregory smiled at Michael's words and then the realization sank in; he knew that he and Michael were safe there to enjoy each other's company.

They sat chatting for some time and yes, Gregory was married and no, Michael was not, but they found themselves attracted to each other. Michael looked over Gregory's body and realized that Gregory was not the ordinary looking man as he might have thought. The man had a tapered body, one that has been worked on in a gym and he had also obviously spent much time out in the sunshine because the tell-tale tan line of a Speedo bathing costume was evident. Michael found this small patch of white skin sexy to look at and found himself becoming turned-on by the older man next to him. He also noticed that Gregory threw the occasional glance at Michael's lithe, athletic build, and he enjoyed being admired.

Their conversation was limited to everyday topics, and at no time did Michael venture near the subject of family or wife, in case this worried Gregory. After their second drink at the bar, Michael felt Gregory's leg press up against his and immediately he felt a rush of blood to his brain which instantaneously sent a message to his groin area where his cock reacted. A gentle pulsing sensation ran through the growing length of his uncut cock and he knew that Gregory had noticed this, because the pressure against his leg increased. Michael watched as Gregory's cock began to swell and rise between his legs. Gregory became a little embarrassed at first and tried to push it down between his thighs, until Michael gently squeezed Gregory's thigh and smiled at him.

"Shall we go somewhere?" asked Michael, his cock now standing to full attention.

Gregory merely returned the smile and nodded. As the two men stood up from their barstools, Michael took Gregory by the hand and led him off to an area behind the bar where it suddenly became darker and where very little was visible, until one's eyes became accustomed to the limited lighting that was available

There were a number of darkrooms, some with beds and others with mattresses on the floor, but Michael never took Gregory into one of these. Instead he continued to walk until he reached a small vacant room with a leather sling attached to the ceiling by thick chains. Michael took Gregory in his arms and began kissing him. Their tongues entered each other's mouth and fought for occupation while their bodies rubbed up against each other, their cocks dueling together.

"What do you like doing?" asked Michael, breaking from their kiss.

Gregory was a little embarrassed and confessed to having never done this with a man before.

"We haven't done anything yet," remarked Michael, "other than kiss. Would you like to make love to me?" he asked.

In the dim light, he could see Gregory's excited look on his face at this thought.

"Yes please," came the almost silent reply.

Michael saw a small table in the corner of the room on which was a container filled with condoms and lube. He crossed to it, picked up a condom pack, tore it open and rolled the condom onto Gregory's hardened cock, the cut head swelling majestically as Michael slid the condom over the top of Gregory's throbbing cock.

"You have such a beautiful cock," said Michael, going down on his knees and kissing the tip of Gregory's cock and then sliding his mouth down its condom-covered length.

Gregory gasped as the warmth of Michael's mouth encompassed his growing length and he gave a gentle thrust, allowing Michael's mouth to reach the very base of Gregory's long stem. Michael continued to manipulate Gregory's cock down his throat, giving Gregory a feeling of absolute joy. Gregory's groans became more vociferous as he held onto Michael's head, forcing his length further down the young man's throat.

Michael released his grip on Gregory's cock and began to manipulate Gregory's pendulous balls into his mouth, one at a time, salivating each and rolling his tongue gently over each. After some time, Michael rose to his feet, kissed Gregory, led him to the sling hanging in the center of the room and said, "Are you ready to make love to me?"

Gregory nodded and smiled, his cock already producing some pre-come which was lubricating the inside of the condom sheath. Michael moved over to the sling, his erect manhood swaying before him as he walked, climbed into it, raised his legs into the air, letting them rest against the chains, tore open a sachet of lube, squeezed some onto his fingers and inserted them into his asshole to lubricate himself. He left his fingers embedded within himself, rotating them gently. Gregory watched, fascinated. Gregory moved to between Michael's legs and he too slid one of his fingers into Michael's twitching asshole. Michael gasped when he felt the extra digit entering him and immediately encouraged Gregory to insert another of his fingers. Both men's fingers began a slow probing, circular motion. Gregory started to slide his fingers in and out of Michael's pulsating rosebud. He watched with interest as each stroke brought pleasure to Michael.

Michael withdrew his fingers leaving Gregory's to create a sense of expectation. Soon he felt the fingers being extracted from his entry. He watched his new-found friend's face as Gregory slowly began his slow but assertive entry into the warm cavity which had been loosened to allow a free and easy progress. Gregory's face was one of expectation, his eyes were focused on Michael's and both men smiled at each other in anticipation of the full, deep entry. Michael could feel Gregory's cock sliding gracefully into him, painlessly. His eyes remained fixed on his older friend. He held his breath until Gregory's cock was fully embedded and could feel his firm balls slap up against Michael's ass, and then he gave a long satisfied sigh.

Gregory held his position once he was deeply embedded in Michael.

"Oh, this feels good," he sighed as he began a slow withdrawal, pulling his cock out until only the tip of his cock was hidden from view. He then gave a sharp thrust, pushing right the way in again, causing Michael to groan in ecstasy. The sling jerked with the sudden jolt and then began a gently, but rhythmic swing. Gregory gradually increased his pace, holding onto the chains where Michael's legs were resting, pulling the sling towards and then away from himself.

Both men were building up a sweat from their actions and both bodies were beginning to glow in the limited light available. Gregory leant forward and placed his lips on Michael's. With each thrust of his cock, Gregory's tongue searched for Michael's, dueling with it each time. The pace of the sling increased, allowing for deep, long penetrations and with each thrust, Michael groaned pleasurably.

A few other men ventured into the small room to watch, but this intrusion did not concern either Michael or Gregory; both men were almost in a trance-like state to worry about others watching their actions.

Gregory indicated that he was getting close to shooting his load. Michael immediately grabbed hold of his own cock, sliding his foreskin back and forth over the sensitive glans, while forcing his throbbing asshole onto Gregory's engorged cock. Suddenly Gregory withdrew from Michael, ripping off his condom in the process and started jerking himself off.

"I'm going to come!" exclaimed Gregory.

Michael increased his speed and was the first to come, covering his slim, firm stomach with his warm love juice. Gregory remained fixed on Michael's now throbbing and ejaculating cock, while be brought himself ever closer. Gregory gave a short, sharp groan, tensed his abdomen and fired the first of many shots onto Michael's face. The stream that followed splattered onto Michael's heaving chest, stomach and cock until there was nothing left for Gregory to milk.

Gregory slid back into Michael's body, both men breathing heavily as they slowly returned to normality, and each one's body becoming coated with their joint supply of warm, white cum.

"If this was your first time," said Michael, kissing Gregory gently on the lips, "then you're very good and I hope that it was as good for you as it was for me."

"I don't know how to thank you," breathed Gregory into Michael's ear, "but I hope that we can do this again some time."

"I would like that," replied Michael, as Gregory's still hardened cock remained throbbing in Michael.

When both had recovered their breath, Gregory slid very gently from Michael's tight ass, helped Michael from the sling and they stood enwrapped in each other's arms, enjoying their combined warmth.

As Michael led Gregory to a shower area to clean themselves, he said, "Next time you come into the bar and ask for a Singapore Sling, I'm not going to be sure whether you want the drink or the actual sling!"

- TEQUILA SUNRISE -

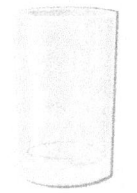

Ingredients:

½ oz Grenadine
4 oz Orange juice
1½ oz Tequila
6 Ice cubes

Directions:

Fill a highball glass with ice. Add tequila and fill with orange juice; stir. Slowly pour in grenadine and let it settle. Before serving, stir.

Very gently once, to create the "sunrise" effect.

TEQUILA SUNRISE

From my hotel room I could hear the waves crashing on the shoreline as I lay staring at the ceiling fan which constantly turned in a slow fashion. I glanced to my left and watched the gentle rise and fall of Miguel's tanned, sculptured chest as he lay sleeping. This was unfortunately my last day in Acapulco and soon I would be leaving him to some other man or woman to enjoy his pleasures. I watched as the athletically defined pecs rose and fell and the stomach muscles expanded and retracted. A thin wisp of dark hair traced a line from his indented bellybutton down to his pubes, and there lay his glory, relaxed, long and foreskin-covered. The glow of the early morning sun was beginning to invade my room and soon Miguel would awaken and I would be departing for home.

I had arrived in Mexico a week earlier and had booked into my hotel in the Avenue Las Conchas in Acapulco. It was a comfortable hotel situated about a two-minute walk from the beach, so every night I was able to be lulled to sleep by the distant ebb and flow of the waves on the shore. There was no reason for my coming to Acapulco other than I wanted a beach holiday somewhere in Mexico. I could have gone to Cancun, but the attraction of Acapulco was to see the divers of Acapulco who leapt from the heights of the cliffs into the swelling seas below, risking life and limb.

The first few days I had done the typically touristy things and had spent much time on the beach catching up on my tanning. On the second last day of my holiday I decided to make enquiries about the divers and where I would be able to see them performing.

The manager of my hotel was extremely helpful and arranged for me to be taken to the spot from where they dived so that I could view the spectacle. He had added a bonus in that I would also be able to take a small boat onto the water below the mighty cliffs and watch from below as the divers entered the sea.

I set off from my hotel and soon arrived at the famous spot where these young men took their lives in their hands to defy the elements of the sea. I was given a position on top of the cliff, along with many other tourists and some locals, to watch the spectacle.

A group of young men, of varying statures, arrived in various shades of Speedos, to the spot where the tourists were seated. I scanned the group of nine men and watched how they oozed charm, chatting to beautiful young women, while they disrobed and revealed their generally chiseled bodies in skimpy Speedos to the oohs and aahs of the women.

My own eyes were not slow in focusing on some of these men. I admired their smooth, tanned skin offset, in most cases, against the colors of their bathing costumes. I also admired the bulges which were evident in the front of most of their Speedos.

Some of their faces were a little weather-beaten and so my attraction diminished, but there was one who stood out among the rest. A tall, darkly tanned young man of about twenty-eight, stood among a group of adoring women, wearing a pale yellow Speedo, his upper body tapering down in a V-shape to a slim waist. His biceps resembled those of a junior body-builder and his upper thighs looked like they could crush a person's body, if the desire was there to do so. I felt myself drawn to this young man, so I joined the thronging women surrounding him.

Their chatter was incessant and he just kept smiling, but I did manage to catch his eye and noticed that the smile he was offering the women, broadened when our eyes met.

A very large Mexican, who I can only imagine must have been the 'manager' of these divers, said something in Spanish and all the young men departed and headed for the top of the cliffs.

Situated near their diving point was a small altar with a cross on it at which each of the divers stopped and prayed, obviously for their safety in the dives. After each had said his prayer, they made their way to the edge of the cliff and watched the swells in the sea below before making their dramatic dive.

Each of the men gave a spectacular dive, entering the sea and resurfacing safely. After each dive, they would climb into a small boat floating nearby and return to a point where they could climb the cliff-face to the top and repeat their dive again for the benefit of the tourists.

I watched in awe as my yellow-Speedo man left the cliff, arms outstretched in the fashion of a swallow and sped through the air. As he neared the surface of the sea, his arm moved to above his head and his slim body slid majestically below the surface of the water. I waited with bated breath until I saw his head rise above the surface. I breathed a sigh of relief knowing that he was safe, then watched as his muscular arms took hold of the rocky cliff and he began the ascent to the top. Seeing him climb made me realize how his arms and legs had become so muscular. He seemed to be climbing with ease, each muscle straining as he went higher and higher until he eventually reached the top again. I watched a few more dives and then requested that I be taken to the small boat to watch from the bottom.

The boat met me and I climbed aboard. There was only the 'skipper' and me in the boat as we headed back to the base of the cliff to await the first of the divers.

Two or three divers would dive one after the other, then swim to the boat to be picked up and taken back to the cliff. As they pulled themselves into the boat, I watched with pleasure as their muscles strained and wondered how envious the women at the top of the viewing area must be with me being in such close proximity to these Latino wonders.

My man, as I now like to refer to him, gave a solo dive leaving the cliff top in a backward position. I watched as the V-shape body sped through the air and at the last moment, straightened out his arms to enter the glassy water. He surfaced and swam to the boat in order to board. As he reached the side of the boat, our eyes met and a smile appeared on his face.

"Hola," he said, water dripping from his face and with his hair slicked back.

I instinctively stretched out a hand to assist him into the boat. He reached for my hand and I felt the strong grip as he took hold. His pull on my arm was so great that I thought he was about to pull me into the sea with him, but instead, his lithe body emerged from the sea and landed in the boat next to me.

Water ran from his smooth body while his wet yellow Speedo clung to his torso. I could clearly see the outline of his long, thick cock helping to create a huge package in the front of his costume. From its outline and shape, it was clear that he was not circumcised, nor was he shy to reveal his length to anyone. He saw me eyeing his crotch and looked down to see the outline of his manhood.

"Eet is small because of thee coolness of thee water," he offered, in his Mexican-English accent.

I stared in wonder as I thought what I saw was not in the least bit small.

"I don't think you're small," I instinctively said, and then blushed knowing what I'd said.

Again he looked down at his crotch, gave his cock a squeeze and adjusted its lie and replied, "Eet gets much beeger when I am not in the water."

With all this talk of cocks and him squeezing and playing with his cock, mine was beginning to take on a life of its own. I looked down at my own crotch and could see how it was tenting my shorts. My diver also noticed this and moved to beside me on the seat on which I was sitting.

"You also look quite beeg," he whispered when he was close enough not to be heard by the 'skipper'. "Where are you staying?" he enquired.

"Near Condessa beach," I replied.

"You want me to come to your hotel?"

What an offer! I was not about to turn down a hunky looking diver who was making a pass at me.

"I smiled sweetly and answered, "I would like that very much."

"I come thees afternoon and if you like, stay the night, yes?"

I could feel myself becoming excited at the idea of this man staying with me for the night.

"By the way, what is your name?"

"Miguel," came the reply.

"I'm Joe," I said, extending a hand to shake hands with him.

"Hola Joe," he said as his huge fingers wrapped around my hand and squeezed. Throughout the squeeze, his dark eyes buried themselves into mine and I was ready to melt into his arms, but the world was watching from the cliff tops.

At the end of the diving display, I managed to speak briefly to Miguel to give him the directions and room number, and headed back to my hotel, leaving him and his friends to the cluster of women who were left behind and who were probably trying to make dates with these men.

Back at the hotel I showered and lay on the bed to relax before my afternoon visit. I must have dozed off because it was a loud knocking which awoke me and I noticed it was quite late in the afternoon. I quickly grabbed a towel from the bathroom, wrapped it around my naked body and went to answer the door.

Miguel stood in the doorway all in white: white t-shirt and white shorts, tightly encasing his firm body.

"Come in, please. I was just having a lie down," I said, trying to explain my disheveled appearance, because my hair had dried in all directions after my shower and having slept on it.

Miguel entered and briefly looked around the room.

"Thees is very nice room, Joe. How long you stay in Acapulco?"

"I'm leaving tomorrow," I replied.

Suddenly a thought crossed my mind. "Did anyone at the reception see you or ask you where you were going?" I enquired.

"Oh no. Eet is fine because thee manager he knows me," came the answer.

That both alleviated my concern and aroused it even more. I wasn't sure what the hotel policy was about having strangers in one's room, particularly after hours, as it was going to be my intention to keep Miguel for the night.

"Would you like to stay the night with me Miguel?" I asked tentatively.

His enigmatic smile said it all.

"Of course!"

"Would you like something to drink?" I offered.

"You have tequila?"

"Sure," I replied, moving to the mini-bar that was in the room to get some mixers. As I stood at the small table in the room, pouring our drinks, I felt Miguel's presence behind me, and then I felt his muscular arms around my waist as he pulled me into his body. I felt his chest and crotch pressed up against me as he began to nibble at my neck. I stopped pouring as my concentration was now waning.

His tongue moved to my ear and soon was licking in and around my ear. Little nibbles were made to my earlobe while I could feel his cock growing ever longer and harder, but then so was mine. He pushed hard up against my ass with his cock and began a slow rubbing of his crotch over my ass. I put my hand behind me and felt the solid length, which I squeezed between my fingers. A slight moan was emitted from his throat.

"You have a nice ass," he whispered into my saturated ear.

I needed him to know how I felt, so I broke free from his clutches and turned to face him. I wrapped my arms around his slim waist and pulled him closer to me so that he too could feel my hard-on and know that what he was doing was turning me on.

I took hold of his T-shirt and pulled it up over his head to reveal his muscular chest. It looked so inviting that I let my mouth move down to his protruding nipples and, taking each one separately into my mouth, began to nibble them. His moans became more voluble and his thrusts more urgent.

I slid my tongue over his tanned, smooth stomach on my way down to his crotch. When I was at eye level with the top of his shorts, I pulled on the waistband and lowered them to his ankles. His cock sprang free and as it did so I noticed a wetness to show that he had been leaking some pre-come.

I kissed the tip of his cock and then taking hold of the foreskin, pulled it over the top. I inserted my tongue and ran it around under his foreskin and pushing it into his piss-slit. Miguel's vocal sounds were rising with each movement I made on his manhood. I slowly pushed his foreskin back until it was right back, revealing his pink glans which I began to wash with my tongue. His cock was thick, but I had no trouble in sliding it down my throat. I sank my mouth down his length until my chin rubbed up against his balls. I sucked on his length and then began a slow withdrawal until his stiff cock popped from my mouth. I knelt before him, admiring his cock which contrasted in color with the rest of his tanned body.

"You have a beautiful cock," I said, licking and kissing all along its length.

"Suck me more," he gasped.

I obliged and once more sank to the depths of his hung balls.

"Thees feels soo good," he murmured, thrusting gently into my throat.

I moved to his well-hung balls and caressed them with my tongue, but when I moved to between his legs and aimed to eat his ass, he clamped my head between his thighs.

I heard him groan and then felt him take me under my arms and lift me. He never said a word, but I gathered that he was not into having his ass attacked in any way.

He kissed me, then he began a journey down my body. The towel that I had wrapped around me when Miguel had knocked on my room door was now lying on the floor so there were no obstacles to overcome as he made his way to my mushroom-shaped cock-head. The suction that he created with his mouth was intense and I thought I was going to shoot immediately. I fought hard not to come too soon as I wanted to enjoy this man's attentions. I stood astride as his mouth searched my sensitive spots. First he found the rim of my cock-head, then he engulfed my balls, and finally he found the strip of flesh between my balls and my waiting asshole. I shivered as his tongue ventured nearer and nearer to my quivering pucker.

The tip of his tongue gently touched my rosebud pucker causing it to clamp shut, but it soon opened up again to his gentle caresses. His tongue ventured along my ass crack thoroughly lubricating me, and then I felt the magic touch of a finger entering me. My body was shaking with excitement as his finger sank deeper into my asshole. I desired more than his finger, I wanted him deep inside of me, pounding my ass with his stiff rod.

"Miguel, please fuck me," I pleaded as his finger probed my innards, but he chose to ignore me.

Slowly, still with his finger embedded in me, he moved me towards the bed, allowing me to lower myself onto my back. Immediately I raised my legs to allow him easier access to me. I could see how his cock was oozing pre-come. I knew what he wanted and I wanted it as well, but for some reason, he was holding out, which was driving me crazy. Again I pleaded with Miguel to enter me.

He gently withdrew his finger from my lubricated and loosened ass, then holding the thick stem of his cock at its base, he rubbed his cock across my ass crack. Every time his cock-head touched my ass hole, my body quivered with anticipation, but still he chose not to enter me. I knew that I wouldn't hold out much more and that I would soon be coming all over myself, so I warned Miguel. He smiled at me and continued his teasing.

I squeezed my cock in the hopes of delaying my eruption, but it was useless. I felt my balls move up towards my stomach, tensed and groaned as I fired the first shot onto my chest. As I shot, so Miguel re-inserted his finger, digging deep into me. My ass muscles clamped tightly around his finger, preventing him for escaping, but he had no intention of doing that; instead he inserted two more fingers, spreading my ass as I fired load after load of warm come.

As my body began to relax, I felt Miguel guide his hard-on into my waiting ass while he continued to keep his three fingers embedded there.

"Aah, yes!" I gasped as he entered me. Although I had come, I felt I needed to be subjected to a powerful pounding from this young man. I wanted his cock thrusting deeply into me, making me quiver with excitement. He had brought me along a highly erotic journey and I felt almost that I wanted to be raped by this man.

As he plunged his thick cock into my warm body, I thrust back to meet his deep thrusts. I wrapped my legs around his waist, pulling myself closer onto his cock. He placed his arms around my back and lifted me off the bed while I was still impaled on his long, thick rod. I wrapped my arms around his neck and rode his stiff cock while his hands spread my ass cheeks wider. As his cock slipped in and out of my throbbing hole, I felt a finger on each hand pulling my ass cheeks apart, slide into my hole. With his hands and his cock working my asshole, I felt myself getting close again.

The tightness of thick cock accompanied by fingers, worked on my prostate and my breathing became heavier and quicker. Miguel knew I was going to come.

"Come baby. Shoot that hot load onto me," he said, grinning with excitement at the fact that I was about to come a second time in such a short period.

I clung on tightly to him, my cock rubbing against his stomach while his cock and fingers brought me closer to a point of no return.

I cried out aloud, shooting onto Miguel and increasing my thrusts onto his length. My balls felt painful from the exertion and my cock throbbed as my come oozed from its tip, lubricating both of us.

Miguel held my ass in his hands and lowered me gently onto the bed once more, without him losing contact with me, still continuing to plunge deeply into my ass. Although I was physically exhausted, this man had energy and at no stage did he show signs of tiring.

He began using short, sharp thrusts, increasing his pace and with it, his breathing. After about a minute of these short thrusts, he gave a deep growl that seemed to come from the very belly of the earth, pushed deep into me, held his position with his balls slapped up against my ass and sent all his pent-up seed flowing into me. He gave a couple more deep but quick thrusts and then fell exhausted across my stomach trying to get his breath back. Once he had recovered a little, he raised his smiling face to me and said, "You one good fuck."

I laughed and as my sweaty face rubbed up against his, I kissed his cheek and said, "so are you, Miguel."

We rolled over onto our sides, him still embedded in me, and fell asleep.

I awoke early in the morning to find Miguel's hand wrapped around my already hardened cock, while his hard-on pressed up against my tight crack. Gently I pushed back onto him and felt his foreskin push back as his beautiful cock slid effortlessly into my waiting ass, and once more we set off on our journey of sexual delight until we again fell into the land of dreams, both having been satisfied.

From my hotel room I could hear the waves crashing on the shoreline as I lay staring at the ceiling fan which constantly turned in a slow fashion. I glanced to my left and watched the gentle rise and fall of Miguel's tanned, sculptured chest as he lay sleeping. I slipped from the bed and crossed to the small table where the night before I had attempted to make drinks for us, but which we had never managed to have. I picked up my tequila and, standing at the open window, watched the magnificent sunrise as my Mexican man slept peacefully.

- **WHITE RUSSIAN** -

Ingredients:

1 part coffee liqueur
1 part milk
1 part Vodka

Directions:

Pour into glass and drink. Works just as well with cream.

WHITE RUSSIAN

The lecture hall filled with the regular students: those waiting to be filled with knowledge, those who attending because they had to, and then those who were simply there to admire the Visiting Professor – that's the category in which Danny Carmichael fell.

Professor Dimitri Andrechev entered the lecture hall and a silence fell over the place. To some he appeared like a bear of a man, but without the hair, while to others he was large, muscular and attractive. Although his intellectual abilities were not to be underestimated, it was his physical appearance which appealed to most. He was probably in his mid-thirties, of medium height with a solid frame. He was always casually, but elegantly dressed, with his shirts and pants cut to enhance his body shape. His upper body was shaped in a v-shape, with broad shoulders tapering down to his slim waist, and his trim hips leading down to well-developed thighs which were evident through the tightness of his well-cut pants.

Those who intended to make a quick getaway after the lecture sat near the rear of the lecture hall, while those genuinely interested in the lectures sat near the front. As for Danny Carmichael, he was in the front row, not because he was academically inclined, nor because he wanted to make a quick getaway.

"Good morning, Ladies and Gentlemen," boomed the deep, resonant baritone voice of Professor Andrechev. "Today we shall be discussing White Russians and their impact on the Russian Civil War of 1918 – 1921."

Danny, who was twenty-years old and had an athletic build, heard the words 'White Russians' but not much else. He sat, as if in a trance, elbows resting on the bench on which his books lay, hands clasping his chin and the sides of his face, while his eyes followed both the face and body of Professor Andrechev. Danny watched as the thick, muscular legs encased in the tight-fitting casual pants carried the professor's solid body across the lecture hall. Danny saw the professor's mouth opening and closing, much as one might see a fish gulping for air, but never heard any words being emitted.

As Danny looked at Professor Andrechev, the words 'White Russian' kept reverberating through his head. In his mind's eye, he slowly unbuttoned Professor Andrechev's shirt, slowly revealing the sturdy, white chest of the Russian with the developed pectoral muscles on which lay two tan-colored areolas from which protruded two enlarged nipples. The chest was hairless, smooth and defined.

Danny thought of his own pale brown nipples and wondered what it would have felt like rubbing his own brown African-American nipples against those of the White Russian. Although Danny was slightly shorter and considerably slimmer than his Russian idol, it still didn't prevent his imagination from conjuring up visions of the Russian holding Danny's chocolate-colored body closer to his white counterpart.

"The White Russians represented the opposition to the Bolsheviks," continued the rich baritone voice, while Danny's mind's eye continued to slowly strip Professor Andrechev of his clothing.

Danny's posture hadn't changed since the lecture began; with the exception of his eyes which followed Dimitri Andrechev's every move.

Danny visualized removing the large Russian's shirt and then undoing the top button of the Russian's beige-colored pants and slowly, very slowly, sliding the zipper down to its base. The front flared open to reveal the white waistband of Professor Andrechev's briefs which had Calvin Klein emblazoned on it in black. Danny's eyes focused on the branded waistband and then moved downward and saw the white bulge of the briefs. He could see how the cotton briefs hoisted Professor Andrechev's hefty balls and cock upwards.

Danny sat entranced as Professor Andrechev's casual pants slid down his hefty legs to reach his ankles and the professor stepped out of them. At this stage, Danny decided to join Professor Andrechev by mentally removing his Bermuda shorts. He sat in his jockstrap, feeling the urge between his legs growing as he watched Professor Andrechev strut in front of him in his briefs.

Danny watched as Professor Andrechev's hefty package moved hypnotically in front of him with each step that he made. As the professor moved away from him, Danny sat in awe as he watched the firm white brief-encased bubble-butt of the professor move sexily. Eventually, Professor Andrechev came to a halt in front of Danny. Danny stared at the heavy crotch that was presented at eye-level. Danny found himself stretching both hands out in front of him, taking hold of the Calvin Klein waistband and lowering Dimitri's briefs, allowing the hefty cock and balls to break free.

Danny's eyes focused on the long, thick, uncut Russian cock that was presented to him. His chocolate brown mouth moved closer to the white appendage hanging, waiting to be taken. His lips touched the tip of the Russian's cock, allowing his tongue to lick that part of the cock-head not covered by the foreskin.

Professor Andrechev's eyes took on a dream-like appearance as he looked down and saw the chocolate mouth begin to engulf his white cock. Danny's mouth and tongue lubricated the solid length of white flesh and as he did so, so he felt Professor Andrechev's foreskin slowly peel back to disclose his smooth, pink cock-head. Danny withdrew his mouth, held the hard stem along which he had traveled with his mouth and admired the pink, rounded head with the wide, gaping piss-slit from which he soon hoped would emerge a shower of warm, white cum. He squeezed the base of the long stem and slapped the Russian's hard-on across his face and mouth.

Danny continued to work Professor Andrechev's cock until he felt the thick, muscular arms lift him to his feet. He felt the large hands rub across his own engorged cock, still encased in his jockstrap.

The professor's fingers wandered around to the back of Danny and he felt the professor slide a finger under the strap at the rear and skim his skin on its journey in search of his pucker. The stubby finger found what it was searching for and Danny waited in anticipation for the entry to take place. Slowly the finger slid into the accommodating entrance and Danny squirmed as he felt the penetration go deeper. After a moment or two of this ecstasy, the professor removed his finger and clasped the wide waistband and pulled Danny's jockstrap to the floor. The long, brown cock with its enlarged mushroom-shaped head emerged, bobbed at being freed and emitted a modicum of pre-come. The professor was not slow in lapping up this love-juice before it dropped to the floor. Danny watched as Professor Andrechev's white lips converged over the throbbing head and sank down the slim stem until his white face was embedded in Danny's dark pubes. Professor Andrechev's cheeks became indented as he sucked long and deep on Danny's chocolate rod. Danny began a gentle pelvic thrust, pushing then pulling his hard-on in and out of the confines of the White Russian's warm cavern.

As the professor slurped on the hard length in his mouth, so his fingers manipulated and caressed Danny's balls, gently moving to massage and rub the area between Danny's ball sac and his pulsating asshole.

Danny felt the White Russian's mouth tighten around his long stem and the Russian's tongue licked around the ridge of his cut cock-head. Danny shuddered with excitement at this tight feeling, and his cock throbbed as he got closer to offloading his juice. He thrust a couple of times, deeply, in Professor Andrechev's throat and then with a gasp, he fired his load, breathing heavily and erratically as he did so. Finally, with his cock dry of its love-juice, Danny gave a deep sigh and relaxed.

"Mr. Carmichael! Mr. Carmichael!" came the deep, rich baritone voice.

Danny suddenly jolted to reality. His dream-like trance suddenly dissipated and he looked around him. The lecture hall was empty except for himself and Professor Andrechev.

"Mr. Carmichael, I do not know whether you have heard a word of what I spoke today, but from what I can see, you appear to have had an accident," said Professor Andrechev, looking straight at Danny's crotch.

Danny looked down and saw a large wet patch covering the front of his shorts. He looked up embarrassedly into the smiling face of the White Russian.

"Maybe you should come with me to my office so that we can discuss today's lecture," said Dimitri Andrechev, taking Danny by the hand and helping him out of his seat and leading him, smilingly, from the lecture hall to discuss the role of White Russians.

When they reached Professor Andrechev's office, Danny was ushered in and invited to sit. The professor closed the door behind him and went to the opposite side of his desk. He sat down and stared at Danny.

"Would you like to tell me about today's lecture, Mr. Carmichael?"

Danny blushed but didn't answer.

The professor leant back in his chair, his crotch coming into Danny's line of sight. He stared at the tightly covered bulge and knew that the professor had indeed got something large in his pants. The professor slowly caressed the bulge, rubbing his hand slowly across the crotch area. Danny's eyes followed.

"Were you thinking about this?" enquired the professor, still leaning back.

Danny, without thinking, nodded in the affirmative. The professor rose from his seat, walked around his desk and sat on the edge of it, facing Danny. In doing this, his pants had been pulled tighter across his crotch. Danny could see that the professor's bulge now had increased in size and that he could also see the outline of the professor's swelling cock. Once again the professor slid a hand across the bulge, causing Danny to lick his lips as he watched. A subtle thrust of the hips was made by the professor and this was all that Danny needed.

Danny rose from his seat, unzipped the professor's pants, pulled them down and hauled the long, thick cock from its hiding place. Danny knew what he wanted to do, so without an instruction or request, he sank his mouth over the stiff piece of Russian meat. Dimitri Andrechev thrust deep down Danny's throat, and although he felt he was going to gag, Danny fought to keep the man's length down his throat. Danny's mouth worked wonders on his lecturer's cock, because it wasn't long and the professor was groaning and thrusting wildly into Danny's mouth.

"Aagh!" groaned Dimitri. "I'm going to shoot!" he exclaimed.

Danny held on firmly, increasing his speed and waiting for the first tastes of Russian saltiness. Dimitri fired a load, which filled Danny's mouth, causing Danny to let go. The second load shot onto Danny's cheek and nose. Danny instinctively opened his mouth as if to catch the last drops, which he did with finesse. He licked his lips and through a come-streaked face, he smiled at his professor, knowing that he'd learnt a great deal about White Russians that day.

- JAPANESE SLIPPER -

Ingredients:

2 parts Cointreau
2 parts Midori melon liqueur
Juice of ½ lemon

Directions:

Shake well with lots of ice. Pour into cocktail glass.

JAPANESE SLIPPER

Mr. Yamoto sat transfixed as he watched the kabuki performance unfolding in front of him and the others in the packed theatre. The stylized performances of the male actors held him entranced; in fact, so entranced was he that he found himself sitting forward on the edge of his seat, not because the show was tense or hair-raising, but rather because he found himself held in the grip of one of the actor's performances.

Although the actor's facial mask may have appeared frightening, Mr. Yamoto was taken in by the voice that emanated from the mask. A soft, yet manly voiced filtered through the air to reach him in his seat. Mr. Yamoto became so transfixed by the actor's performance, that he almost forgot that he was watching acting and began to immerse himself in the plot.

The show came to an end to well-deserved applause, and Mr. Yamoto sprang to his feet as he wanted to acknowledge the wonderful performances and also wanted to go back stage to congratulate the cast and in particular, the person playing the character that had enthralled him.

For obvious reasons, it took some time the actors to remove their make-up and costumes. After some time, Mr. Yamoto was permitted to knock on the dressing room door of the actor he so desired to meet.

The door opened and there stood a handsome, clean-faced, young man in his mid-twenties, dressed in a royal blue kimono and wearing royal blue slippers. Mr. Yamoto bowed graciously to the young man, who returned the gesture.

"May I speak to Mr. Yuuichi?"

"You are speaking to him," replied the young man.

Mr. Yamoto's expression was a one of shock. He hadn't expected to find such a young man playing the character. He stood staring into the young man's smiling face.

"I apologize, Mr. Yuuichi. I did not expect someone so young to have such masterful skills to portray your character."

"Thank you for your compliment, sir."

"I apologize once more, Mr Yuuichi for not introducing myself properly. I am Mr. Yamoto."

"How do you do, sir," bowed Mr. Yuuichi. "Please won't you come in?"

Mr. Yamoto entered the dressing room and was offered a seat. Both men sat, Mr Yuuichi facing the mirror on the wall in front of him, and Mr Yamoto behind him, facing into the mirror.

"I must congratulate you on your wonderful performance, Mr. Yuuichi. I enjoyed it thoroughly, so much so, that I will definitely return to see it again."

Mr. Yuuichi smiled and bowed his head slightly.

"Thank you; you are most generous in your praise."

Mr Yamoto smiled at the clean, young, open face that smiled back at him in the mirror. Mr Yamoto became somewhat coy at not knowing how to continue the conversation, but he found this young man attractive and didn't want to excuse himself of Mr Yuuichi's company just yet. The young man could see his visitor's predicament.

"Mr Yamoto, may I ask if you are here alone tonight."

"I am Mr. Yuuichi."

"In that case, I would be honored if I could invite you for a drink."

Mr Yamoto's face was a mixture of puzzlement followed by relief, followed by joy.

"It would be my honor," he replied.

"Let me dress and I will join you outside, if you wouldn't mind," continued Mr. Yuuichi.

Excitedly, Mr Yamoto rose, followed hastily by his new young friend; they bowed to each other and as Mr Yamoto began to leave the dressing room, he noticed, in the mirror, how Mr. Yuuichi's kimono fell open to reveal a trim, muscular and tanned body, devoid of any body hair. He stared long and hard at the young man's torso before realizing that Mr Yuuichi was also staring admiringly back at him. Mr Yamoto also noticed the taut, white briefs that Mr

Yuuichi had on under his kimono, and smiled, bowed and exited the dressing room.

Mr Yuuichi slid the kimono from his body and stood admiring himself in the mirror. Yes he had a beautiful body; one that he'd taken good care of by eating properly and exercising regularly at the local gym. He then slipped on a pair of beige cotton longs and a white shirt, combed his straight dark hair, smiled once more at his image and opened the dressing room door. Mr Yamoto was standing waiting for him.

"I have my car outside if you have no transport," said Mr. Yamoto, leading the way out of the theatre building.

They both walked together until they reached the car. Mr Yamoto opened the passenger door, allowing Mr Yuuichi to seat himself, then carefully closed the door behind him and went around getting behind the driving wheel.

"Where would you like to go for a drink?" asked Mr Yamoto.

"I really don't mind," replied his young companion.

"Would you like to come back to my apartment?" enquired Mr. Yamoto.

Mr Yuuichi nodded and smiled, so they headed towards the Shinjuku area where his apartment was situated. They passed a number of brightly lit bars and clubs, until they finally reached Mr. Yamoto's address. They parked the car and caught the elevator up to the fourteenth floor.

Mr Yamoto's apartment was simply yet lavishly furnished and it was clear to the young man that Mr Yamoto lived alone. On the wall hung some beautiful artworks reflecting Mr Yamoto's interests in aesthetic objects, and scattered around the room were statues of both male and female figures made of a number of different natural media. From the large lounge windows, one could see the twinkling lights of Tokyo spreading for miles around, illuminating the sky.

Mr. Yamoto invited his young guest to take a seat, which he did in a two-seater couch facing the large lounge windows, while Mr. Yamoto busied himself pouring them each a drink, then, after passing Mr. Yuuichi his drink, sat in a chair opposite the young man.

The two men, whose ages together wouldn't have added to more than seventy, sat smiling at each other. Mr. Yuuichi took in the good looks of his host who looked very much like a typical Japanese businessman, in his opinion. Mr. Yamoto was not tall, but then neither was Mr. Yuuichi, and had a stocky, almost muscularly well-defined shape. Mr. Yuuichi could see through Mr. Yamoto's shirt that the man had a well-developed upper body, the type that would be gained from attending a gym regularly.

"Tell me about your character," said Mr. Yamoto, after a time of smiling and saying nothing.

"What's there to tell," replied his younger visitor, "other than I enjoy playing the part."

"Do you find that you identify with your character, at all?"

"I don't think so," replied Mr. Yuuichi. "In fact I think that some times I'm the opposite."

"But your character seems such a gentle soul. Are you telling me that you are not like that?"

"Not entirely. I think I'm a gentle soul, but I think that if I'm pushed too far in certain situations, I might not be that gentle soul anymore."

Mr. Yamoto looked a little concerned by this statement, not quite sure how to respond.

"Your character falls in love with the lead woman but in the end, hates her because of his perceived ideas that she's been unfaithful to him and then he kills her. Don't you think that the character might have been more open to finding the truth about his wife rather than just killing her because of his suspicions?"

"You mean, shouldn't I have questioned matters first rather than jumping to conclusions?"

"Yes, exactly."

"Probably," replied Mr. Yuuichi, "but I had no say in how the script should be written."

"Mr. Yuuichi, would you as a person, and not as the character, have questioned the wife first rather than just killing her?"

"I probably would have, yes."

Mr. Yamoto smiled at this answer, and then added, "May I ask whether you are married, Mr. Yuuichi?"

Mr. Yuuichi smiled broadly at his host.

"Mr. Yamoto, I am not."

"Ah," sighed Mr. Yamoto, "perhaps that is good as then you have no wife to kill, should you feel that she's been unfaithful to you."

This all seemed a very odd thing to say, but Mr. Yamoto was not stopping there. He had finished his drink so rose from his seat, ventured towards the drinks cabinet and poured another drink for himself and Mr. Yuuichi.

"Sir, a Japanese Slipper cocktail," he said handing the glass to his guest and settling himself down on the two-seater couch alongside of Mr. Yuuichi.

The young man slid a little way along the couch to allow his host to sit. Once the host was seated, he slowly slid a little closer to his younger guest until their legs touched. Mr. Yamoto gently placed a hand on his guest's leg, but Mr. Yuuichi never rejected the touch. The older man's hand slid a little closer up his younger guest's leg until it was almost on Mr. Yuuichi's crotch. Mr. Yuuichi calmly sipped his Japanese Slipper from his glass and watched as the hand encompassed his crotch. A gentle sigh emitted from Mr. Yuuichi as his host squeezed a little harder. Mr. Yamoto smiled at his young friend. Mr. Yamoto could feel his young friend's arousal growing and this pleased him. He gulped down his cocktail, placed his glass on a side table and turned to his friend.

"You want to see my room?" he asked, rising from the couch.

Mr. Yuuichi smiled and bowed, placing his glass down and also rising from the couch. The older man led the younger to the bedroom, which also had magnificent views across the city.

Gently and with great care and attention, Mr. Yamoto undressed his young guest until the young man stood only in his white briefs, his erection clearly visible. The host stood back and admired his young friend in the room lightened only by the outside lighting. Slowly he lowered Mr. Yuuichi onto his back on the double bed and then lay on top of him, his own erection desperate to be released from his clothing. The two men lay smiling at each other, until Mr. Yamoto's mouth found his visitor's and their tongues began a duel.

Mr. Yuuichi rolled his host over onto his back and began to undress him until the older man lay naked on the double bed. Mr. Yuuichi stared admiringly at the taut, muscular body. This was definitely not what he would have expected of a Japanese business man. His host must have some other occupation. To have acquired such a body.

Mr. Yuuichi's white briefs were soon removed from his body and then both men began to 'search' the other's body. They made love, caressing each other and almost worshipping each other as they did so. After a night of passionate love-making, Mr. Yuuichi rose from the double bed exhausted, dressed and quietly left his hosts apartment.

For five nights in a row, Mr. Yamoto visited the kabuki theatre to watch Mr. Yuuichi's performance, and after each performance, the young actor would return to his older lover's apartment and each night they would drink a cocktail together and then ritualistically make love to each other.

This behavior continued for two weeks, but during that time there was an evening when Mr. Yamoto waited outside the dressing room after the show, but when Mr. Yuuichi emerged, he said that he wouldn't be able to accompany his older host as he was going out with someone else. Mr. Yuuichi departed in the company of someone around his age while Mr. Yamoto was left standing outside the theatre, lost, not knowing what to do. For a moment he stood watching as the car carrying the two men drove off, and then he hailed a taxi cab to follow the young men.

They drove towards the Shinjuku area and stopped outside a brightly lit club. The young men parked their car, alighted from it and entered the club. Mr. Yamoto did likewise. When he entered the club, he was met by loud music and many people dancing. Although the venue was brightly lit, he took some time to adjust to the light and then he began a search for Mr. Yuuichi and his friend. He slowly made his way around the club, searching in all the dark nooks and crannies, but couldn't see them. He was about to give up when he noticed Mr. Yuuichi on the dance floor. He stood staring at the young man who was dancing almost in a trance-like state with his friend, neither of whom noticed Mr. Yamoto.

After standing and watching the two men for some time, the music ended and the two young men went off to a darkish corner together. Mr. Yamoto followed. In the darkened corner, he could see how the Mr. Yuuichi fondled his equally young friend, which aroused Mr. Yamoto. The young men's hands traversed each other and as they searched each other's body, so Mr. Yamoto became more sexually excited until he couldn't contain himself any longer. He walked to where the men were.

"Wouldn't you like to come back to my place, both of you?"

Mr. Yuuichi half recognized the older man, but he was obviously drugged with something and fell up against the older man. Mr. Yuuichi's friend also seemed drugged and began to fondle Mr. Yamoto, much to his delight.

"Let us go back to my place where it's more private and the three of us can have some fun together," said Mr. Yamoto, trying to pull both young men towards the exit door.

After much persuasion, the two young men agreed to go with Mr. Yamoto. They all got into Mr. Yamoto's car, leaving the other car outside the club, and drove back to the older man's apartment.

Back in the apartment, both men were given a Japanese Slipper cocktail to drink while Mr. Yamoto slowly undressed each of them. Once both young men were naked in the lounge, he began to arouse each of them by making sexual advances to them; sucking them and groping their cocks until they both had erections. He then encouraged them into his bedroom where the three of them sprawled out across the double bed, making love.

Mr. Yamoto slid his hard cock into Mr. Yuuichi as the young man's mouth warmed his young friend's cock deep down his throat. They kept these positions for some time until the young friend groaned loudly and shot his load down Mr. Yuuichi's throat. Mr. Yamoto was not long in holding back and was soon firing into his young lover. No sooner had this occurred, than they changed positions and continued to please each other.

After what seemed an eternity, both Mr. Yuuichi and his young friend fell asleep, exhausted from their sexual activities, leaving Mr. Yamoto also tired, but awake. The muscular older man quietly rose from the bed, went into the lounge to fetch something and returned. He then went into the bathroom and brought back with him a towel. He laid the towel on the bed alongside the two sleeping men, then he picked up the item which he'd brought from the lounge, and in the light reflected from the twinkling Tokyo lights, one could see the long, shining blade of a samurai sword.

"It is sad when you are unfaithful to the one you love. It is sad that you didn't learn from the part you played in the theatre, because had you taken that role more seriously, none of this would have to happen, but if I cannot have you to myself, then no one shall have you," said Mr. Yamoto, lifting the glinting sword high and plunging it into the sleeping body of Mr. Yuuichi.

There was a grunt and a groan and then silence.

Mr. Yamoto went back into the bathroom, put on a kimono-style dressing gown and a pair of royal blue slippers similar to those that Mr. Yuuichi had worn in the play, returned to the bedroom, knelt on the bed next to his young friend's body, held the point of the sword against his muscular stomach and slowly sank his taut body onto the length of the blade.

As the blade sank deeper into him, this military man released his soul to join that of Mr. Yuuichi's. The two men's bodies lay side by side on the bed, their hands touching, while Mr. Yuuichi's friend lay innocently asleep, unaware of the tragedy which surrounded him.

- MAI THAI -

Ingredients:

1 oz Light Rum
½ oz Dark Rum
½ oz Amaretto
1 oz Pineapple juice
½ oz Triple sec
1 oz Sweet and sour mix

Directions:

Mixed together with crushed ice in a glass and garnish with mint leaves.

MAI THAI

I left the refreshingly cool, tranquility of the hotel foyer and stepped out into the oppressively sweltering heat of Pattaya, Thailand. It was midday, so it was naturally hot, especially as it was their summer, but the heat seemed to be sapping, resulting in my T-shirt clinging to my chest ten minutes into my walking. My pecs and nipples protruded through the saturated material of my T-shirt, while my gently rippling six-pack appeared like tiny waves through the material.

I had decided to take a walk in order to have some lunch, but didn't expect the intensity of the heat. I wandered along the beach road, seeking shade where possible, but not finding much. Thinking that there might be more shade available by heading away from the beach and going more towards the shopping areas, I wandered up one of the narrow side streets.

As I made my way along the street, dogs, cats and even humans seemed to be sparse, and those who were seen, seemed to be in a lethargic mode, lounging in whatever shade could be found. I rounded a corner and noticed three young men sprawled out on couches in the shade. Two of them seemed half asleep, but the third, on seeing me, leapt from his couch, stretched out a hand to shake mine and said, "Hello" in a sing-song intonation. Being friendly, I clasped his hand and felt him pull my sweaty body to his.

"You want to come inside?" he intoned in the same sing-song mode, hugging me to him.

As politely as I could, I said that I didn't want to join him inside the empty bar, but he continued to persist. He was shorter than me and I could feel his crotch pushed up against me and then felt his cock rubbing against my thigh and beginning to get hard. He continued asking me if I wanted to join him, while his two friends lay in the shade looking completely bored.

I continued to resist, but his hands began feeling my pecs and nipples through the saturated material, then he ran a hand over my crotch. I could feel myself getting hard, but I didn't want to encourage him too much, as he was not my type of guy, so I suggested that I might see him later in the evening if I decided to go for a drink.

He agreed to this and I managed to free myself of his clutches and continued my journey. I found a cool, air-conditioned mall, entered and found a restaurant to have something to eat.

After eating lunch, I wandered around the mall surveying what the shops had to offer and checking out the men. I walked past a water feature next to which sat three young Thai guys, chatting. As I walked past, I noticed one of them, a rough looking guy, glance at me. I continued wandering about and then headed towards one of the toilets in the mall. I was standing at the urinal when I noticed, out of the corner of my eye, the rough-looking guy enter and stand next to me. He unzipped and pulled out, what can only be described as, a pendulously, thick, cut cock of substantial length. We stood together, cocks in hand, both getting harder, as we made eye contact.

The situation was awkward, as the toilet was busy and there was nowhere to go. I watched as his Thai cock grew longer and thicker as he slid his coarse hand along its length. I immediately copied his action and between eye contact and smiles, we both got harder and harder. As I looked at him, I realized that nothing was going to happen between us, so I stuffed my hard-on back into my shorts and left my hustler Thai guy.

Although I had got myself worked-up a little, I wasn't ready to have a quickie, so to speak, so I wandered on, checking out the guys I passed on the streets. No one's looks jumped out at me and I was beginning to wonder if there were any Thai guys that I might be attracted to.

I had been aware that most S.E.Asian men were short and basically looked pretty, rather than handsome. It was this fact that made me realize why so many Thai men could get away with dressing and looking like a woman; they did it with finesse.

I wandered into what is commonly termed as 'Boyz Town' and although it was early afternoon, when nothing much happens because of the intense heat and most people being found on the beach, I was surprised to round a corner and find seven young men, all dressed in white shorts, vests, with white shoes and socks, together.

The typical Thai friendliness came forth as each of the seven smiled at me and greeted me in their broken English.

They were seated at tables, which occupied a hotel's verandah, and alongside them was a placard advertising various forms of massage. That seemed a good idea, I thought.

I stepped up from the hot street onto the cool verandah and spoke to a white-clad young man.

"Can I get a massage?" I asked to no one person in particular.

"Go to counter," said one, pointing to another young guy in a green shirt.

He pointed to a list of different types of massages, among them, oil, cream, foot and full body. I pointed to the oil because I fancied a slippery massage. My next task was to choose a masseur.

The seven young men stood together, each smiling at me a little more than the one next to him. It felt like a meat-market to me, but probably to them, they were used to this method. I really felt for the guys who had neither looks nor body to win them much favor.

I surveyed each face, but there was only one that stood out from the crowd. I also noticed that accompanying the good-looking young face was a trim, muscular body with well-formed biceps and sturdy, solid legs. The sight was imprinted on my mind, but I continued to survey the remaining faces before me. When I had completed the surveillance, I approached the good-looking young man and said, "I would like you, please."

He thanked me for choosing him while the others went back to their seats and continued chatting as though there had been no interruption to their lives.

I followed my new young friend and the green-shirted man, who took my money for the massage. We waited outside of an office while a room key was collected, and then my young friend led me up a steep flight of stairs, along a narrow passage until we reached the selected room.

When we entered, there was a bed against a wall, a small table alongside of the bed, a mirror along the wall by the bed, a shower, a toilet and a small rug on the floor.

Throughout the introductory phase, my Thai friend showed politeness, courtesy and respect. We introduced ourselves and he told me his name was Kao, which in English means 'nine', so I wasn't sure whether each of the young men was merely given a number and in Thai that becomes their 'working' name.

Kao handed me a towel and suggested I shower while he readied the bed and placed the oil on the side table. When I had showered and dried myself, he asked me to lie on the bed on my stomach while he showered. As he undressed, he kept his back to me and although slim, I could see that he must work-out regularly. Once he had showered and dried himself, he placed his naked body at my feet, rubbed oil onto my left foot and leg, and began massaging.

"Where you from?" he enquired as he massaged my toes and feet.

I told him and asked if he was from Pattaya.

"No, from Chiang Mai."

"How long have you been doing this here in Pattaya?" I asked as I felt my calves being manipulated and watched his muscular, young body in the mirror.

"Three years," came the reply.

"You have a very nice body," I complimented, as I felt his hand reach my upper thigh and massage over my ass, then slide his hand down my ass crack.

"Thank you," he answered.

I continued to watch Kao in the mirror as he stretched across my body from my feet to my lower back. I felt his hard cock rub against my leg, so I knew that we were on equal grounds. My cock throbbed as his hands manipulated my ass and then I felt his hand slide between my legs and his oily fingers grasped my hard-on and began lubricating it. As he did this I instinctively raised my ass to allow him greater access to my balls and cock. His oil-slicked hands slid easily along my length, causing a warm feeling in my groin.

Kao then began the entire process again on my right leg. His touch was so erotic that I was beginning to want him to touch the rest of my body. He must have sensed my feelings because soon he was once again rubbing his hardened cock over my ass crack. Again, I raised my ass to meet his movements. He continued rubbing himself against my bubble-butt, but I soon felt him rubbing oil over my upper back. Once he had completed doing this, he began sliding his entire body over mine.

His chest slid seductively over my back, his oily hands holding onto my shoulders as his cock searched for my asshole. I felt his hard-on slide over my ass and across my ass-crack, and then I felt it slide between my legs and prod my balls. I felt myself getting harder with each thrust that Kao made.

He continued his slow, seductive sliding, searching for my hole, but before he found it, I wanted to look into his face, so I rolled him over onto his back and let his oil-covered chest, stomach and cock rub across mine.

Our mouths met and I spread my legs so that I could wrap them around Kao's waist and pull him closer to me. His muscular chest and small nipples rubbed across my protruding nipples, causing me to puff out my chest.

I began sucking on Kao's nipples, hoping to get them hard. I then moved down over his ripped abs and found his long, cut cock just waiting to be taken. I held its base and sank my mouth down his length until my chin rubbed against his oil-covered pubes.

Kao groaned incessantly as my mouth and throat took his cock and clamped pressure on it. Gently he held my head as he began a slow upward thrust as he fucked my throat. Kao had small balls which I gently massaged with my finger tips until I reached a stage where I wanted to suck on them too.

As my mouth left Kao's cock and headed for his balls, he swung his body around so that we were now in a 69 position, his mouth clamped firmly around my cock while I took both his balls into my mouth and ran my tongue over them.

After some time, I went back to Kao's mouth to kiss him.

"What do you like doing, Kao?"

"Can I fuck you?" he asked, smiling at me.

"I'd like that," I replied, turning over to lie on my stomach as I had been when we started.

Kao resumed sliding his whole body over mine as his cock once more searched for my entry.

"You have a condom?" I asked.

I felt Kao adjust his position and watched in the mirror as he slipped a condom over his oil-slick hard-on and then resume his search.

I raised my ass to help him make his entry. When I knew that he was at my entrance, I thrust upwards, impaling him in me. We both gasped as he sank deep into me, and then he began a slow, long, rhythmic fuck. We both writhed against each other remaining attached, while his right hand took my oil-slick cock and started jerking me.

There was a feeling in me that I didn't want to come in the position that we were in, and I realized the desire to see this beautiful, taut, young body in action.

Without losing contact, I rolled onto Kao so that he was on his back once more, then I sat up and slowly swiveled on his cock until I was facing him. We smiled into each other's face as I began to rise and fall on his weapon. I leant forward to lick and nibble his nipples, tightening my ass muscles as I continued to ride him.

Kao's breathing and moans were becoming more intense as his oily hands slid along my shaft, bringing me closer to shooting my load.

"Be careful Kao. You're getting me close."

Although Kao released his grip on my cock, he increased his thrusts deep into my waiting ass as he brought himself closer to releasing his seed.

I sucked continuously on his nipples, chewing them gently as he continued thrusting deeply into me, pounding his balls against my ass. My hand went down to his balls and I caressed them gently, sliding a finger into myself at the same time, feeling the ridge of his stem sliding in and out of me

His hand resumed their position on my cock and soon his movements along the length of my cock were increasing in speed, so I knew that he was also getting near to coming.

"Kao, you're gonna make me come," I gasped.

This didn't stop him. His sound effects increased in volume and so did his thrusts. My ass was taking a Thai pounding as both our bodies dripped with oil and perspiration. My mouth found his and our tongues dueled together while ass and cock connected.

I couldn't hold out any longer. I gasped and warned Kao that I was about to shoot. With his eyes closed, stomach muscles tensed, he cried out and thrust deeply into my ass at the same time as my cock spurted my warm cum onto his muscular chest. His hand slid along my cock length, mixing cum with oil as he continued to thrust into my depths and as I clamped my ass tightly around his throbbing cock. We were both gasping from exertion, his muscles tensing and contracting with each ejaculation, just as mine was doing.

The noise from both of us as our bodies clashed with each other was excessive. As our bodies began to relax and return to a form of normality, I leaned across Kao's body, my lips touching his, our eyes smiling at each other, and felt the gentle throbs as his cock emptied itself. I lay on top of him for some time, not wanting him to leave my warm confines. I tightened my ass muscles to prevent him from sliding free and continued to grind my ass on his length.

Finally, Kao slipped from the warmth of my ass's grip and we lay smiling into each other's face.

"That was beautiful," I whispered as we lay looking into each other's eyes, and my hands wandered across his muscular back and down to his taut little ass.

"Thank you," replied Kao, gently fondling my balls and subsiding length. "You have lovely ass. Nice and tight," he continued, letting a finger slide beneath my balls and finding my entry once more. I gasped and smiled happily as I felt his finger being inserted into me again, in search of giving me pleasure.

After a moment of glowing together, while his finger teased my innards, we kissed, rose from the bed and showered.

We showered once again; dressed, hugged each other, smiled and then I left him in his room, no doubt preparing for his next customer.

- BLUE HAWAIIAN -

Ingredients:

1 oz Blue Curacao
1 oz Coconut Cream
2 oz Pineapple juice
1 oz Light Rum

Directions:

Fill a blender with 3 oz crushed ice and all the ingredients. Blend the ingredients at a low speed for about 15 seconds or until smooth. Pour into a Highball.

BLUE HAWAIIAN

I had met 'Surfer Boy', as his e-mail name said, on the internet, having found this young man's e-mail address on the back of a washroom toilet door amidst a variety of other graffiti. It had never occurred to me before to take much notice of what was written on toilet doors, but somehow this day I took notice. Again, why I chose to focus on 'Surfer Boy's' e-mail address, I don't know.

I sent a rather non-descript message and awaited a reply. I imagined 'Surfer Boy' to be slim, sun-bleached blonde and tanned; all the stereotypical aspects one associates with a surfer. I soon received one and from him and then our messages grew until I received a picture and a full description of 'Surfer Boy'. Here was a good-looking, twenty-six year old surfer man with a bronze tan and a broad smile. No, he wasn't completely blonde, but had some blonde streaks in his hair, and he wasn't as slim as I might have expected; he was more muscular, particularly in his upper body.

A few weeks later I received another picture of 'Surfer Boy', but this time it wasn't a head and shoulder shot; 'Surfer Boy' was depicted in his wet suit. His body was encased in a pair of tight rubber wet-suit shorts and an equally tight wet-suit top, unzipped in the front to reveal a smooth, tanned, muscular chest. I looked admiringly at the picture and wondered if we'd ever meet or in fact whether he really wanted to meet me.

I sent back a message after seeing 'Surfer Boy' in his surfing gear, telling him how cool he looked. Immediately, more pictures arrived showing 'Surfer Boy' with his top off, with his wet-suit shorts rolled down to below his belly button, of his crotch and slim legs, in fact every type of picture of 'Surfer Boy' except a full-frontal nude shot. I became excited with each picture and found myself thinking what a good fuck-buddy "Surfer Boy' would make, if he were interested.

My problem with meeting 'Surfer Boy' was that we were both only able to meet at odd hours because of my working and his surfing.

We kept up a constant e-mail, writing about things in general such as his surfing and my ordinary life. At no stage did either of us make any mention of a sexual nature, but I was definitely interested in meeting up with him. The e-mails continued and he sent me pictures, but I never received any nude photos of him, although I would have longed to have received one. Finally I decided the only way that I was going to meet him was to say that I would be interested in learning to surf, something I had never considered before.

I sent an e-mail suggesting my interest in surfing and asked whether he'd be interested in being my 'teacher', so to speak. A reply came back with the words, "Can't wait."

"When can we start?" I wrote back, desperate to meet him.

"Have you got a board?" came the reply.

Of course I didn't. I hadn't thought of that so I replied, "I thought I might try yours."

'Surfer Boy' replied, "I'd love you to ride mine."

On receiving this message, I wasn't sure as to what he was referring. I noticed the word 'love' and immediately became suspicious. Why would someone like a surfer use a word like that, especially to another man, I wondered? Then I thought of the words 'ride mine'. Was he referring to his surf board, or was there some other subtle suggestion being made. My sex-starved brain began to wander. The thought of possibly riding his Hawaiian cock excited me, if that's to what he was referring.

"When can we get started?" I sent back.

"How about this coming weekend?" came the response.

"Saturday 2 p.m. OK with you?"

"Meet me at shopping mall near the beach – top floor," came the answer.

I immediately became puzzled. How on earth was I to learn to surf on the top floor of a shopping mall, but maybe he was going to meet me there and then take me to the beach.

On Saturday morning I pulled on my jeans and T-shirt, threw my swimming costume into the car and set off to the mall. By 1 p.m., I was already wandering around the shopping mall, looking for 'Surfer Boy', but no sign of him.

At 1.45 p.m. I made my way up to the top floor, where there were a few shops but many offices, which were closed over the weekends. I wandered aimlessly, staring into shop windows, until I spotted a tall, muscular looking guy in Bermudas and a T-shirt, heading towards the washroom on the top floor. Could this had to be 'Surfer Boy'?

I followed, entered the washroom and saw the tall, tanned young man standing at the urinals. I moved to stand next to him. I unzipped, pulled out my cock and then looked at the face next to me.

"Surfer Boy?" I asked

He looked back at me. "Hi, Chad?"

"Yes," I replied, smiling into his blue eyes.

My eyes automatically left his face and went down to his cock, which lay flaccid in the palm of his hand. It was long and tanned like the rest of his body, uncut with a tight foreskin and I could see his pubes were shaved. I immediately wanted to grasp this luscious appendage, but something prevented me. As we stood staring and smiling at each other, my cock took on a mind and a life of its own and began growing in girth and length.

"That looks good," said 'Surfer Boy', smiling at the situation in which I was finding myself. My cock got harder by the seconds as he stood looking down at my length, and now I could see that 'Surfer Boy' was following suit.

"Let's go into the cubicle," he suggested, heading towards the toilet at the end of a row of four cubicles.

I followed, neither of us tucking our cocks away.

When he had secured the door, 'Surfer Boy' dropped his Bermudas to his ankles and sat on the toilet seat and leaned back.

"You said you wanted to ride my board, well here it is," he said, holding the base of his hard cock firmly.

I had the urge to take his length, so I immediately knelt in front of him in an almost worshiping position and covered the tip of his cock with my mouth. Using my lips, I slowly pushed back his tight foreskin until the smooth, pink head was revealed to me, then I inserted my tongue tip into his piss-slit, licking there and around his cock-head until his cock-head glistened. My mouth and tongue played with his head and stem, then I nibbled at his foreskin. I eventually widened my mouth and slowly took him deep down my throat.

His groans were softly audible and I glanced up at his serene face as he sat there; his eyes were closed as if in a dream-like state with his head thrown back.

After some time of lubricating his length, I stood up, removed my jeans, pulled out a condom from my back pocket and unrolled it down his throbbing cock. As I did this, he gave me a knowing smile of approval. Once it was securely in place, I stood astride his legs, faced him and slowly lowered myself onto his full erection, guiding it into my warm confines. His face was a picture of concentrated pleasure as I sank down on him. Both of us exhaled a simultaneous gasp as my ass came to rest on his lap, his stiff cock firmly embedded in me. We smiled into each other's eyes and I began a slow rhythmic rise and fall action. He held onto my hips, lifting and dropping me onto his length, while I slid my hands under his T-shirt in search of his nipples. I felt two hardened, well-formed protrusions which I pinched, causing him to thrust deeper into me each time I squeezed them. I continued to do this as I enjoyed the deep thrusts he was giving me.

We remained in this position for some time, stopping only when we heard the washroom door being opened. When that occurred, I would teasingly wriggle my ass on his cock and pinch his nipples while we tried hard to remain silent. Once the person had departed, we resumed our action with soft sighs and kisses.

To vary our position, 'Surfer Boy' wanted to stand up for a while, so I rose from his lap, turned around and leaned against the toilet door while he re-inserted his throbbing cock from behind. This time he took hold of my cock which had been dribbling pre-cum all the while, and using this, lubricated my whole length, his hand sliding effortlessly along my hard cock. This slickness was bringing me closer to my climax and I warned him.

"So am I, Chad!" he exclaimed, pushing harder and deeper into me.

Suddenly I emptied my load over his hand and the toilet floor, while I felt the rhythmic throbs as he ejaculated into me.

Once we had come down from our heady ecstasy, I released him from the tight muscular clenching that my ass muscles had on his cock, and he slid gently from my grasp. We dressed and hugged each other and kissed tenderly.

"Do you often do this?" I ventured to ask.

"You mean fuck guys?"

I nodded.

"Quite often," was his reply.

"If I had to see you walking in the street, I would never have thought you were into guys, but I'm glad that you are," I smirked as I said it.

As we left the washroom together, I asked, "Why did you suggest meeting here?"

He laughed, and with a glint in his eye, replied, "I find doing it in a public place, like a toilet, exciting and dangerous, much the same way that surfing is."

"Talking of surfing, when are we going to have our first lesson?"

"You've already had it," he laughed. "One of the most difficult things to master in surfing is staying on the board, and I can vouch for the fact that you certainly know how to get comfortable on a board and how to work it. All you have to learn now is to handle it while lying on the board," he chirped.

I grinned from ear to ear on hearing this because I couldn't wait for our next 'lesson'.

As we left the mall together, I knew that I had myself a future fuck-buddy, but whether I would ever get to learn either his real name or how to surf properly, would remain a mystery

- HARVEY WALLBANGER -

Ingredients:

½ oz Galliano
4 oz Orange juice
1 oz Vodka

Directions:

Pour vodka and orange juice into a Collins glass filled with ice and stir. Float Galliano on top by pouring slowly over a teaspoon turned bottom-side up.

HARVEY WALLBANGER

The crystal champagne glasses clinked together making a refreshingly high-pitched sound, while the open French doors allowed the gentle breeze to infiltrate the room causing the crystal chandeliers to join in the melodious sounds as they swayed in the breeze. People mingled happily, chatting above the sounds of glass, and enjoying the event – the twenty-first birthday of Harvey Quinton-Smythe, socialite, wealthy son of the industrialist Benjamin Quinton-Smythe and heir to the Quinton-Smythe Empire.

Harvey had led a sheltered, spoilt life and never needed for anything, thanks to his parents. He was also an only child, which made his upbringing all the more materialistic in nature. His friends were from the same upper class circles and so they understood each other's backgrounds. Harvey had gone to a private school and then started college, where he spent two years before dropping out. Rumor has it that he couldn't cope academically, but Harvey's excuse was that he found it all very boring. Be that as it may, Harvey had decided to spend time doing nothing at home for about six months until his father suggested that he join the business so that he would have some knowledge of it when he inherited the position of president of the company from his father.

Harvey, although still young, had an air about him, which suggested a far greater maturity. He had gone to gym while much younger and had developed a significantly well-built physique which, together with his good looks and cropped brown hair, acted as an attraction to most of the equally wealthy young women with whom he came into contact. In fact, Harvey was considered a woman's man; attracted to all the young women and they to him.

Having come from a family where he was encouraged to debate issues and talk about current affairs, made him appear more mature than his actual years. The result was that he could mix freely with adults just as well as he could with younger people, and although he was accepted openly in adult company; he was equally comfortable in younger company. In particular, Harvey had two very close male friends, namely Josh Greenberg and Michael Smith, both of whose parents were high-flying businessmen.

Harvey, Josh and Michael, who were also all the same age, were often seen attending society parties, film premiers and other celebrity functions together. They would also go out drinking together, where on many an occasion, it would his two friends who would have to make sure that Harvey returned home safely after over-indulging too much. It was also during these drinking sprees that Harvey took on another persona. It was almost as though during the day he was Dr Jeckyl and at night he became Mr. Hyde. His behavior patterns varied with each occasion.

The first time that Harvey noticed any difference in his behavior was one evening when he'd gone out alone, as Josh and Michael had other dates and couldn't make it. Harvey had driven himself to an up-market restaurant for a meal and a quick drink, and then headed off to a bar in downtown Los Angeles. He drove around for a while before arriving at the bar, but it was during his driving around that he noticed that something about him was changing. At first he couldn't explain the feeling that he was undergoing, but as he drove past hookers and hustlers, he noticed an urge to stop his car and speak to one of these people, but then, on the other hand, he despised them as they were, in his view, lower class and below his standards of living. He looked at the variety of men and women who frequented the streets, some very attractive in a rough sort of way, while others remained unavoidably unattractive. A number of both men and women, smiled as the car drove slowly passed, Harvey, noticing each one's features. He couldn't explain to anyone, should they ask, why he was doing this. For at least twenty to twenty-five minutes he drove around surveying the 'talent' on the streets before heading to his planned destination.

In the bar, which was fairly crowded with people like himself, out for a good time and moneyed, he ordered a couple of drinks and then decided to have a relatively early night, so he climbed back into his car and headed home.

On the way home, he felt the need to use a toilet, so he pulled up to a bar he'd never visited before, parked his car and ran in to go to the toilet. There was a urinal and four stalls. He entered one of the stalls, pulled down his jeans and his briefs and sat down. He glanced to his left and right and on both walls either side of him he noticed glory holes, the one on his right, bigger than the other. While he was sitting there, he heard someone cough as he entered the toilets. He glanced through the glory hole on his right hand side and noticed the blue jeans of someone being lowered and then seeing the thighs of the person. He didn't want to be seen peering through the hole, so he glanced away. After a moment, he turned towards the hole again and noticed that the person next door was stroking his cock, which had grown in both length and girth.

Harvey became aroused by the sight from next door to him, but had never endeavored to do anything with a man before. However, having said that, it didn't take Harvey long to become infatuated by what he saw, and soon his own cock was growing in dimensions. Instinctively, Harvey rose from where he was sitting and without so much as an invitation, thrust his hard-on through the glory hole. Instantaneously, a warm mouth surrounded his length and began to lubricate it. This feeling that he was enduring began to drive him crazy with lust, so much so, that he started fucking the mouth on the other side of the wall, until he shot his load into the waiting mouth. When he had finished, he pulled up his briefs and jeans, flushed the toilet and just before leaving the stall, he bent to peer through the hole. There he saw a hunky looking guy of about thirty with a three-day growth of beard smiling back at him. Embarrassedly, he fled the stall, made for his car and headed for home.

Harvey never said a word of his experience to anyone, not even to his closest two friends.

One week later, Harvey was back at the bar where he had seen the bearded guy, but this time for a drink.

The bar was a mix of young and older men, some dressed fashionably while others remained loyal to the jeans and T-shirt brigade. Harvey positioned himself at the bar, but where he could see who ventured to the toilets, in case he had the urge to follow. As he stood at the bar counter, nursing his beer, which in itself was out of character for him as he stuck to cocktails, he noticed his bearded 'friend' from the toilet stall, enter the bar and head towards the toilets. Harvey waited a moment and when the young man never returned, he placed his glass on the counter and headed into the toilet. On entering he found only one stall occupied and the rest of the toilet empty. He moved to the stall alongside the occupied one, closed the door and dropped his jeans. This time he peered through the glory hole straight away and saw his 'friend' sitting there

The young bearded man was leaning back as he sat, with a full erection and was rubbing his hand over the head of his cock and groaning softly to himself. In no time, Harvey's cock was standing to attention, so he did likewise. He thrust his cut cock through the hole and felt a warm hand encompass it. This warmth was soon followed by the young man's warm mouth, which made Harvey gasp with pleasure. Suddenly the mouth disappeared and Harvey felt something being done to his erection. He waited a moment and then began to withdraw it from the hole. As he did so he noticed that the young man had slipped a condom onto his cock. This he took to be a signal of what was required from him. He thrust his cock back through the hole and waited.

A tightness enveloped the head of his cock as his 'friend' from next door, slowly sank his ass onto Harvey's now throbbing cock. Once the young man was comfortably accommodating Harvey's length, Harvey began a slow but rhythmic back and forth thrust. Both men moaned softly with each thrust until Harvey began to speed up his actions. A loud gasp followed by a whimpering emitted from Harvey and the young man next door felt the warm cum filling him.

On completion, Harvey withdrew his cock and ripped the condom from it, allowing the remaining drops of cum to drip onto the floor. He cleaned himself, pulled up his jeans, bent to the hole, smiled at the young man, then flushed the toilet and emerged from it.

"You sure give a good fuck," said the bearded man when he emerged from his stall. "I'd like to meet you again if that's at all possible."

Harvey didn't respond, but smiled warmly to the young man.

"Do you come here often?" asked the young man.

"Not actually," replied Harvey, trying to avoid too many questions.

Harvey washed his hands and departed as hurriedly as he could. He made his way back to his drink on the counter and downed it in one gulp. He then hurried from the bar and hit the streets in his car. What he had experienced was fun for him. This was a first for him, but he enjoyed it. In fact he realized that he was not only becoming a woman's man, but also a man's man. However, he couldn't explain this sudden change, and it only seemed to happen when he'd had a couple of drinks. During the day when he wasn't drinking, he never noticed men at all.

Harvey's visits to the bar became regular and each time he met someone in the toilet stalls and enjoyed their company. This went on for a couple of weeks until he changed his pattern of behavior once more. This time he ventured along the streets where he'd spotted the hookers and the hustlers. He drove slowly by, surveying the men and women who frequented the streets. He saw two guys who attracted his attention but wasn't sure which he preferred. Then he suddenly realized that he couldn't pick either one up, as he had nowhere to take them as he lived at home with his parents. Harvey became a little despondent, until he thought of his bar. Maybe he could take one there for a drink and who knows might happen.

Harvey drove around the block and when he returned to where the men were, he noticed that the two whom he fancied were busy talking to each other. He slowed down next to them.

"Looking for some fun, sir," said the taller of the two.

"Are you two together?" asked Harvey.

The two hustlers looked at each other, then the shorter of the two nodded his head, "Sure we are," came the reply.

"Would you like to come for a drink?" enquired Harvey.

Again the two men looked at each other. This wasn't exactly what they had in mind, but what the hell.

"Sure, why not."

The two men climbed into the car with Harvey, the taller in the front while the shorter climbed into the back. Harvey drove them to his bar, where the three alighted and entered. The two hustlers seemed comfortable with the bar, so Harvey thought that perhaps they frequented it regularly. He ordered drinks for his guests and the three settled down to a quiet chat. Harvey managed to find out their names, that they were Hank and Fred, that is, if that was their real names.

Fred was the taller and more muscular looking of the two. However, that was not to say that Hank didn't have what appeared to be a trim body. Fred appeared about to be in his mid-twenty's while Hank looked young, perhaps even Harvey's age. While they chatted, getting to know each other, Harvey was careful not to divulge his background to the two young men, in case they decided to rob him, he thought.

After half an hour of chatting and drinking, Harvey made a suggestion.

"Do you want to come to the toilet?" he asked.

Both young men seemed surprised at this invitation and therefore didn't respond.

"You see, I can't take you back to my place because there're people there, so I thought we could go to the toilet here. I think you'd like it."

Fred was the first to rise and move towards the toilet, followed quickly by Harvey and Hank. When they entered, the place was empty and Harvey went straight to one of the stall, in fact it was his favorite on, and closed the door, but didn't lock it. He stood and waited. Nothing happened, so he gingerly opened the stall door and peered out. Hank and Fred were standing looking at the occupied stall, bewildered.

"Go next door," whispered Harvey.

Fred went in and closed the stall door, leaving Hank in the main toilet area. Fred peered through the glory hole and saw Harvey playing with his crotch. He knelt watching with interest as Harvey got himself harder and then unzipped his jeans, allowing them to drop to the floor.

Fred liked what he saw, because Harvey had been blessed with a substantial length, so he placed his mouth close to the hole, suggesting that Harvey push his cock through the hole. Harvey obliged and Fred met the length of solid muscle that protruded into the adjacent stall with his mouth.

Hank could hear the slurping sound that Fred was making as he sucked long and hard on Harvey's long appendage. He could feel his own cock becoming aroused by the sounds he heard and the thought of what was happening behind the closed doors. Hank moved to the stall on the other side of Harvey's, climbed onto the seat and peered over the three-quarter wall to see Harvey's cock thrust through the glory hole. Harvey's body was up tight against the wall and he was breathing heavily with each deep suck that Fred was offering him. Harvey turned his head at one stage and saw Hank. He nodded as if to indicate that Hank join him in the stall, so he did.

Hank opened the door to Harvey's stall and quietly entered. He unzipped his tight jeans to reveal a long, thin uncut cock, the foreskin about to roll back completely. Harvey pulled away from the hole and turned to face Hank. Harvey knelt in front of the young man and took his length into his mouth and began sliding along the stem with his lips. Fred, who was still kneeling looking through the hole, watched excitedly as his companion was given a blowjob. He then slipped a hand through the hole and began fingering Harvey. On feeling this intrusion, Harvey adjusted himself so that he got closer to the hole, making it easier for Fred to go deeper. Harvey and Hank's groans were now no longer quiet and their breathing was also heavier.

Fred pulled a condom from his jean's pocket and unrolled it onto his thick cock. He spat into his hand and lubricated his cock-head, preparing himself for attack, then he pushed his thick, long cock through the glory hole and waited. He felt someone's ass nudge his cock tip and then felt a hand hold his stem as it was guided into a tightly warm cavity. As Fred sank into the warmth, so a deep guttural groan came from the stall next door, and Fred began to push deeply into the tight ass that was accommodating his length.

Harvey bent over allowing his 'intruder' more access and at the same time, taking Hank deeper down his throat. They remained in these positions for a while, each groaning and moaning with ecstasy as they brought each other closer to their climaxes.

Fred 's cock swelled and his pendulous ball rose slightly as he throbbed and fired into Harvey's tight ass. Harvey felt the jerks and throbs, which turned him on and encouraged him to increase his pace along Hank's cock. Harvey felt Fred removed his still hard cock from its warm position, but that didn't stop him from working on Hank. Just then the stall door opened and Fred stood there, cock in hand.

"Get next door, Hank."

Hank did as Fred told him.

Fred pulled another condom from his pocket and handed it to Harvey.

"Roll that on and fuck the hell out of him; that's what he likes," said Fred, returning to the stall in Hank had gone.

As Harvey dressed his cock, Fred turned Hank around so that his ass was facing the glory hole, then he knelt and worshipped his young friend's bobbing cock.

Hank felt the thickness of Harvey's cock intrude his body. At first he resisted, but soon gave in and allowed Harvey's length to go deep inside of him. As Harvey pounded into Hank, so Fred obliged by bringing his friend closer and closer.

"Aaah," shouted Hank, after a short while. "I going to shoot!" he exclaimed.

His ass tightened around Harvey's length and milked the industrialist's heavy supply of hot cum from his throbbing man-meat. Hank fired shot after shot into Fred's mouth as he tried to swallow as fast as he could. Some of Hank's love juice escaped and trickled down Fred chin. When he felt the shots subsiding from Hank, Fred licked the top of Hank's rosy pink cock-head, cleaning it for him, then he stood up and returned to the stall in which Hank and Harvey were. All three stood looking at each other as they tried to gather their breath.

"Wow, I've never had anything like that before," said Fred, smiling now at Harvey.

Harvey pulled his slowly subsiding cock from Hank and when Fred saw its length he said, "Next time, I want that thing banging me, but exactly like we did tonight."

Harvey continued to live his 'double life' without divulging his night escapades to Josh and Michael, until one fatal night.

Harvey went off to his now regular bar where he'd become quite renowned in the toilets. He entered, ordered a drink and surveyed the crowd who were chatting and drinking. Nothing out of the ordinary attracted him, so he ventured to the toilets. When he entered, he noticed two stall occupied, but not two next to each other, so Harvey ventured into the empty stall between the two occupied ones. He unzipped and sat down. He cast an eye in both directions to see if he could deduce who was sitting on either side of him, but was unsuccessful at seeing the occupant's faces. However, he was able to see that on both sides, sat men with erections, gently feeling themselves to maintain their erections. Harvey immediately set to work, getting himself hard. It didn't take him long as he was extremely horny knowing what was happening on either side of him.

As he sat there, a thick, short cock was pushed through the glory hole in the wall. He took hold of it and started jerking it. A sigh was heard from the stall. Through the adjacent hole appeared an eye, watching what was happening. Soon a long, thick cock with a bulbous mushroom-shaped head slid through the adjacent hole. Harvey now had a cock through both walls to play with. He took one in the left hand and the other in his right and jerked furiously.

After a moment, the bulbous head, disappeared and a finger was thrust through the hole, suggesting that Harvey insert his cock through the hole, which he did. The mouth that found it swallowed his length down to its base, causing Harvey to gasp at the pleasure he had been given. So intense was his pleasure that he started fucking the mouth that was eating his cock. His hips pounded into the wooden stall wall. From the other hole, a face appeared to watch, then an arm was stretched through the hole, in search of an ass to finger. The hand could just reach Harvey's ass and felt its smoothness. Harvey's pounding through the hole was becoming intense, as though he was getting close to coming, so he pulled out and sat down. The long, bulbous headed-cock reappeared and this time Harvey gave it a mouth cleaning; letting his tongue salivate along its length and then swirling his tongue around the fat cut head. When Harvey took a break from sucking on this deliciously long pole, he noticed the adjacent hole now had an ass facing him, as an invitation. He never hesitated. He ripped out a condom, pulled it on and as the owner of the ass gasped, so Harvey ploughed right in. Once more the wood walls vibrated with their action and the face from next door watched.

A cry emanated from the stall as the guy who was being fucked shot his load onto the concrete floor. The guy in the adjacent stall watched as Harvey's ass muscles clenched and relaxed as he pounded into the other guy's ass; then he stretched his arm through the hole to tap on Harvey's ass. Harvey turned to look and saw the eyes watching him, and then a new ass appeared at the adjacent hole. The guy with the large cock wanted to be screwed, so Harvey obliged. He pulled on a new condom, pushed his cock through the hole in the opposite wall and the guy with the big dick slide his tight ass onto Harvey's waiting weapon. Both men groaned as Harvey sank deeper and deeper into the young man's ass until they both felt comfortable, then Harvey started pounding the wall again.

There was no gentleness here, but brute animalistic fucking taking place through the hole in the wall. Both men were grunting and heaving as they neared their climaxes. Harvey fired first, continuing to pound into the young man's tight ass, then he pulled out. The young man spun around, thrust his cock through the hole into Harvey's side and fired his load. Both Harvey and his first guy watched as the bulbous mushroom-shaped head bobbed as the warm, white cum shot out over Harvey's leg and then onto the floor. As the young man's firing began to subside, Harvey couldn't help but taking this beautiful thick cock in his mouth and sucking it dry.

All three toilets flushed at the same time and all three doors opened simultaneously. Out of the three stalls stepped Michael, Harvey and Josh. When they saw each other, there was a moment of embarrassment, until they saw the funny side to their situation, and burst out laughing.

"Shit, buddy," said Josh on seeing Harvey, "You sure get carried away when you're fucking, hey! I reckon we'll have to nickname you 'wallbanger'; I'm surprised those walls are still standing by the way you hit them with those hips of yours. But tell me, how long has this been going on with you? We didn't know you were into guys!"

Harvey blushed somewhat and explained his Jeckyl and Hyde feelings, but admitted to both Michael and Josh that they could call on him any time they needed servicing, even if it were during the day time.

- ITALIAN DELIGHT -

Ingredients:

1 oz Amaretto
½ oz Orange juice
1½ oz Cream
1 Cherry

Directions:

Shake all ingredients (except cherry) with ice and strain into a chilled cocktail glass. Place a cherry on top and serve.

MILAN MODEL

It's not everyday that one gets a free air ticket to Milan, Italy, or an invitation to attend the International Milan Fashion Week, but here on my desk in a large envelope lay the details.

The organizers of the Milan Fashion Week had decided to incorporate a competition for the male models taking part and I had been invited, in my capacity as a recognized fashion journalist, to be one of the judges. At stake for the models was a contract with a leading American agency, a substantial cash amount as well as photographic spreads in at least two leading fashion magazines.

I thought this would be an exciting break from the everyday routine of writing, so I was only too happy to accept the invitation and begin packing.

On my arrival in Milan, I was met at the airport and driven to my hotel. On booking in, I realized that all the male models were also staying at the same hotel, as there were attractive young men everywhere.

After being booked in to the hotel, I was met by the organizer of the Fashion Week to discuss my role in the judging competition. On the Monday we, the judges, were going to meet the models informally at a lunch around the hotel swimming pool, while on Tuesday and Wednesday we would be having individual interviews with each model. Obviously, during each evening's fashion show, the models would also be judged, with the final result being announced on the Friday night.

At the Monday lunch, we, the judges, were not officially introduced to the thirty-two men aged between nineteen and thirty-one who made up a variety of nationalities.

The models were relaxed, tanning, swimming and just generally lounging around the pool. Without exception, they were all pleasing on the eye. Each was confident of himself and his body, yet each had a type of vulnerability about him in one way or another.

There were Speedos and shorts, sunglasses and caps, tall men and lean men. I wandered around the pool area as if looking for somewhere to place my own towel and things. I found a spot under a shading palm tree, stripped down to my Speedo, oiled my body with suntan lotion and lay back to listen to and observe the thirty-two models. The other judges were doing likewise without anyone being aware that we were judges.

I decided to take a swim, so dived into the pool, swam under water to the other side of the pool and surfaced. As I wiped the water from my eyes, I was presented with a glowing eyeful. Before me, on a pool lounger, lay a tanned young man in a tiny canary yellow Speedo. Our eyes met and I saw a deepness in his, yet they also resembled soft puppy eyes. His lips were full and he had the characteristic Roman nose, a feature common among Italians.

My eyes travelled down his smooth, chiselled chest and came to rest on an enormous bulge covered by the yellow Lycra. I looked in wonder at the heavy package that this young man carried. He knew where I was looking because he subtly rested a hand on his crotch and I noticed how he gently pushed down on his package. My own package began a life of its own. My hands slid under the surface of the water as I adjusted the lie of my swelling cock and watched the yellow bulge also begin to grow.

As I pulled myself from the water onto the side of the pool and stood up, my hard-on was evident and the young man in the yellow Speedo smiled broadly at the sight. Just then, another young man greeted my smiling friend.

"Hi, Bruno. How're you doing?"

"Fine, Mike," replied the young man in the yellow Speedo. "So you eventually woke up," he laughed. "When I left the room for breakfast, you were still in the land of dreams," continued Bruno.

It became clear to me that these two young men were sharing a room at the hotel, and as Mike dropped the room key onto the table next to the pool lounger, I noticed that their room was next door to mine.

I lay on my pool lounger and watched as Bruno continued to eye me and continued placing his hand seductively on his crotch, squeezing it every now and again. Occasionally I noticed that Mike threw a glance in my direction, so I wasn't sure whether they had realized that I was one of the judges.

Mike was also slim with a swimmer's body but not as defined as Bruno's. He had fair hair, was also smooth and had eyes that sparkled when he smiled or laughed.

I wasn't sure whether Bruno and Mike were merely roommates, sharing a room, or if there was something more to their relationship.

Lunch was announced, so I pulled on my shorts, moved over to where the buffet lunch was being served and began mingling with the crowd. I was just placing some potato salad on my plate when I felt a taut body pressed up against me from behind. It didn't disturb me, but I was intrigued to know whose long, hard cock was pushing up against my ass.

"I'm sorry to push into you like that," said a sexy, Italian voice behind me.

I turned my head and came face-to-face with a smiling Bruno, who was standing with an empty plate in his hand.

"Potato salad?" I asked, offering my plate.

I turned to face him and as I did so, I glanced down at his yellow Speedo. His long, thick cock was erect and very evident to all.

"Thanks," smiled Bruno, taking my plate. "Would you care to join us at our table?" asked Bruno, his puppy-dog eyes melting into mine.

"Thanks, that would be great," I replied, having taken Bruno's plate and filled it with some food.

Once we had both gathered food and something to drink, I followed Bruno to where he was sitting, to find Mike reserving a table for him.

"I'm sorry, I don't know your name," said Bruno wanting to introduce me to Mike.

"Hi, I'm Pete," I said, extending my hand to Mike.

"Hi there. I'm Mike and this is my room mate, Bruno."

I smiled at both men and shook Bruno's hand, which clasped mine for what seemed a little longer than normal. We sat down and started to tuck into our lunch.

"Are you connected to the Fashion Week?" asked Mike.

"Hm," I responded, having stuffed my mouth with some food. I swallowed it rapidly and continued, "I'm a journalist for a fashion magazine."

Bruno immediately began to show interest and leaned closer to me, his arm touching mine.

"Which mag?" he enquired.

I didn't want to give my real identity away, so I feigned a fashion magazine's name. Both men looked a little puzzled, but I soon changed the topic and focused on them. As they told me where they came from, I felt a slight nudge as Bruno's right leg brushed up against my left leg under the table. I didn't react by looking at him or removing my leg from the close proximity of his, but the pressure against my leg intensified, so did the arousal in my shorts. I was beginning to feel a little awkward because I felt sure that we shouldn't be fraternizing with the competitors to this extent.

As I sat chatting to the two young men about their careers and fashion in general, Bruno's leg remained 'attached' to mine, when I suddenly felt a hand rest on my upper thigh – it was Mike's. For a moment I froze, not knowing what to do as I found both men very attractive and Bruno in particular, I found extremely sexual. I knew I couldn't allow myself to be seen favoring these two men, so I made an excuse that I had to go and write a report on the Fashion Week to be submitted to my magazine. Whether they believed me or not, I don't know, but I did know that I was going to regret what I was doing.

I thanked them for their company, wished them luck for the Fashion Week and went up to my room to have a cold shower.

At the evening's first show, I watched with fascination at the professionalism of all thirty-two young men. They carried themselves well, used the clothing to their advantage and all told, seemed to be thoroughly enjoying themselves.

After the show, I returned to my room and sat having a nightcap while I reviewed each of the models I'd seen earlier.

I picked up my drink and wandered out onto my patio. It was cool and quiet outside, but as I stood there looking up into the clear night sky, I thought I heard sounds coming from the room next door to mine. I leaned around the wall dividing my patio from next doors and in the bedroom I saw the lithe, naked bodies of Bruno and Mike.

I watched as Mike knelt in front of Bruno, his head bobbing back and forth as he slid his mouth along Bruno's long, thick cock. I could see how Mike pulled Bruno's foreskin over the tip of his cock and then insert his tongue, and then he would slide Bruno's foreskin right back, revealing the pink/purple cock-head, waiting to be licked and kissed.

Instinctively, my hand went down to my own hardened crotch and I began sliding my hand over the outside of my jeans that I was wearing. I eventually unzipped my jeans and extracted my throbbing hard-on, spat into my hand and slicked up my cock.

When I next looked into my neighbor's room, I could see Bruno standing at the base of the bed with Mike's legs held high in the air. From Bruno's movement, I could tell that he was ploughing his hot cock into that hotter ass of Mike's. The sounds of flesh slapping against flesh and groans and gasps with each thrust, was impacting on me. I watched in awe at the prowess of the young Italian. I had heard stories of how Italian men made great lovers and this looked and sounded like just the thing I needed, but there was nothing I could do about it other than to shoot my load onto the patio floor. As my ejaculation subsided, I watched with envy as Mike continued to groan as Bruno delivered the final deep thrusts before both men's levels of ecstatic emotion burst forth.

I left them to their gentle moments of coming back down to normality, and headed back into my room.

Tuesday was pretty uneventful, other than I and the other judges had to interview the first sixteen models on a one-to-one basis. Neither Bruno nor Mike was among the first batch, but there were some interesting young men.

That evening I once again attended the fashion show, which included one designer's beachwear, which allowed me the pleasure of seeing thirty-two half naked men parade before me. From a physical perspective, judging these men was proving difficult as each had a well-toned body, a good healthy tan and it was only the sizes of the packages that varied. For myself, I must confess that size was very important and there were quite a few who never let me down.

When I returned to the hotel after the show, I chose to leave all the lights in my room off and undressed in the dark. I was hoping I might get lucky with a second performance from Bruno and Mike.

I stepped out onto the patio and peered around the dividing wall. Their bedroom light was on and illuminating their patio, but I didn't see either of them. Each patio had a lounger similar to the ones found around the swimming pool, so I casually lay down on mine in the warm night air.

It wasn't long before I heard whispering coming from the next-door patio: Bruno and Mike must be back.

I never moved until I heard the soft moans come floating from next door. I quietly rose from my lounger and neared the dividing wall. As I peered around the wall, I could clearly see another model, whose name I had learnt was Christof, from France, riding someone's cock as that person lay on their lounger. Christof had his back to me but from the available light, I could see as he rose to the tip of the other guy's cock, that this solid piece of flesh was long and thick, so I assumed it was Bruno.

Again my naked body reacted and I started rubbing and tweaking my nipples, allowing my cock to grow longer and harder.

While I was watching Christof enjoy riding Bruno's cock, Mike emerged from the bedroom onto the patio. I immediately ducked so that he wouldn't see me.

I heard Christof groan loudly which caused me to resume my voyeuristic position. Mike had pushed Christof's upper body forward so that he was lying across Bruno's chest, but still firmly impaled on Bruno's good length. Mike was now standing behind Christof and astride Bruno's legs, and I could see he was attempting to enter Christof and join Bruno in that tight ass. As Mike slowly pushed his cock into the tight opening alongside Bruno's, Christof cried out and I squeezed my hard-on.

Bruno and Christof held their positions as Mike sank slowly into the warm confines of Christof. Once he was deeply embedded, both he and Christof began their thrusts. Soon all three men were groaning with joint pleasure as both Bruno and Mike plugged Christof.

I watched, wishing that I was in Christof's position, that it was I who was being pounded by those two handsome men, but it didn't stop me enjoying the sight until I couldn't contain myself any longer and gasped out aloud as I fired my pent-up load. I didn't care if the neighbors heard me because I had thoroughly enjoyed their exhibition, especially as all three came at the same time.

Wednesday was spent in the hotel conference venue interviewing the remaining sixteen models. When Bruno approached the table at which I sat, he smiled profusely.

"I couldn't say anything to you, Bruno," I tried to explain.

"You didn't have to. Mike and I have known you were one of the judges from day one," he replied, lazing back in his chair and spreading his legs wide, allowing me complete viewing access to his inviting crotch.

I needed to focus on the interviews, but Bruno was taunting me and making it very difficult for me.

"How would you describe yourself?" I asked, watching for any facial reactions.

"An exhibitionist," he retorted, without hesitation.

I smiled at his answer, thinking about the two previous evenings.

"So you feel quite comfortable parading in front of people, wearing whatever you're asked to wear?"

"Absolutely," came the confident reply.

I asked a number of other questions relating to modeling and fashion and then asked Bruno if he had any questions.

I noticed how he smiled at me and let a hand slide across his crotch.

"As a judge," he asked, "how do you feel about watching models at work?"

I wasn't sure whether Bruno was referring to my voyeuristic behavior for the past two nights or whether this was a legitimate question relating to fashion shows and modeling.

"I enjoy it very much, otherwise I wouldn't be doing what I'm doing now," I replied, as best I could.

"How would you feel about being like a model, doing what we do in front of others?" asked Bruno.

"That depends…," I answered.

"… on what?" retorted Bruno.

"On whom I was doing it in front of," I continued.

Bruno's smile spread enigmatically across his face. I wasn't sure if my answer was what he expected, but as I had nothing more to add, I thanked him for the interview and let him go so that I could recompose myself before the next contestant arrived.

On Thursday, the other three judges and I met to discuss the candidates. Although each model had something unique to offer, there were five that we concurred were in a class of their own. We decided that at the Thursday evening's show, we would focus specifically on the top five, and then make a final decision on Friday morning. Bruno and Mike were both among the top five, which made my task all the more difficult.

After Thursday's show, I left immediately for the hotel and went straight to my room. I took a shower, dried myself and lay down on my bed, all in the dark. I didn't want anyone disturbing me while my thoughts were on the five top models.

I must have dozed off, for how long I don't know, but a knocking on my bedroom door awakened me. I went to the door, forgetting I was naked, and opened the door. Outside stood Mike and Bruno.

"May we come in?" asked Bruno.

I was still half asleep, but invited them in.

"Let me get a towel or get dressed," I said, heading towards the bathroom, but Mike caught my arm.

"Don't bother, because we don't mind," he said, pulling his T-shirt over his head to reveal his sculptured chest.

"What did you think of the show tonight?" asked Bruno, leading me to my bed and pulling me onto it next to him.

"As usual, I thoroughly enjoyed you guys.'

"Well, we're here to let you enjoy us guys even more," replied Bruno, as he pushed me onto my back on the bed and immediately headed for my flaccid cock.

I felt his warm mouth encompass my limp cock while his tongue licked my cock-head. Soon I could feel myself getting hard in his mouth. Mike started giving my balls a tongue washing as I tried to reciprocate these two young men.

Both Mike and Bruno peeled off their clothes and the three of us rolled around on the bed, each 'attacking' the other. The only way I can describe Bruno and Mike's attention to pleasing me was one of ecstatic euphoria. They made love to every part of my body. Their hands, mouths and bodies caressed and explored every erotic spot in my body, creating a sense that was driving me crazy; I wanted them inside of me, in the same way the had been with Christof.

I whispered in Bruno's ear, asking him to take me. I think he was waiting for that invitation because a grin broke on his face and "only with pleasure" was whispered back into my ear.

I felt Mike slide into me while Bruno fed me his long, thick cock to suck on, then Mike withdrew and Bruno took his place.

My bodily emotions were rising rapidly, but they reached a climax as I felt both Bruno and Mike slowly slide into me together. The initial pain was felt, but this soon turned to pleasure as the two models let me enjoy them more.

The night was long and busy, but as the sun rose early the following morning, and with a model on either side of me in my bed, I was very confused whom of the two to vote for.

At the meeting of the judges on Friday morning, the problem was taken out of my hands as each of the judges had voted for Bruno, so he would be the winner.

During the after-party on the Friday night, I saw Bruno go to each of the judges to thank them for voting for him. As he thanked each, I noticed how he was kissed and hugged by each judge. When he approached me, I asked if he knew each judge personally by the way he reacted with each.

He smiled, hugged me and whispered, "yes, but your ass was the best by far!"

- ADAM & EVE -

Ingredients:

4 ice cubes
4 tsp Brandy
4 tsp Gin
4 tsp Curacao triple sec

Directions:

Shake all the ingredients together, then strain into a cocktail glass.

METAL MEN
AND MARBLE WOMAN

Prague is one of those cities one should visit in one's lifetime. It seems to be blessed with a history and architecture unsurpassed by any other Eastern European cities. I remember seeing pictures of the city in travel brochures and staring for some time at its beauty. The inevitable photos were of the famous set of bridges that cross the Vltava River; the most famous and picturesque bridge being the Charles Bridge or as it is known in Czech as Karlův Most. Its beauty revolved around it being so old yet so majestic with its statues. If one stood at Hradčany Castle on the hill and looked down across the river, the old stone bridge with its statues contrasted beautifully with the red-topped buildings.

I had come to Prague, not only to see its beauty as a city, but I had heard that it was also a culturally vibrant city. There were concerts and operas, ballets and plays, art exhibitions and leisurely boat cruises on the river. In fact, there was something for everyone.

I was sitting, one afternoon, on a bench on the embankment of the river adjacent to the Smetana Museum when I noticed a young man in his early twenties standing watching me. I didn't find him obtrusive in any way, but wondered why he seemed to find me so fascinating. I turned my attention to watching some of the cruise boats plying their way along the river, when I felt a presence next to me. I looked to my right and found the young man standing near me. Our eyes met and he smiled at me.

"You speak English?" He enquired in his own version of broken English.

"Yes," I replied, returning the smile.

He moved a little closer until we were within touching distance.

"You like my city?"

"Oh do you live here?" I asked, rather stupidly.

The smile turned into a beaming grin. Obviously he was proud to say he lived in Prague.

"You like I show you around?" he questioned.

He seemed friendly enough and I didn't think that I was about to be mugged or hijacked, so I agreed to be shown around. He said his name was Pavel, which was easy enough for me to remember; so Pavel and I soon set off along the bank of the river until we reached Charles Bridge and then headed towards the old town.

To describe Pavel would be to describe a young version of Arnold Schwazenegger. He was well-built, with a broad chest and slim waist, as evidenced from the tautness of his shirt as it attempted to cover his buffed pectoral muscles which resembled two large hamburger patties. He had finely chiseled cheekbones and a cleft chin, which added to the attractiveness of this young man.

As we walked, I noticed that the old town, with its cobbled streets, was a maze of interesting small streets going in all directions. We wound our way through the city going deeper into the center until we reached a street with a park running down its middle called Václavské Nám. The name didn't mean anything to me, but as we neared a section of the park, Pavel pointed to something ahead. I stared and caught sight at what he was pointing. There must have been a group of ten metal men. This is the only way that I can explain it: they were statues of men, made out of metal. They looked rough hewn in their structure and this gave them an air of inflexible masculinity. I looked on in awe at each one. There was a rugged sense of power in each sculpture and it amazed me that whoever had made them had given each an element of individuality, yet all had the same ruggedness. It amazed me how they resembled something out of a science fiction film along the likes of an Arnold Schwazenegger-type movie: they were muscular in their shape and naked, revealing every muscle, definition and appendage.

"You like?" enquired my tour guide, smiling profusely as he pointed to the naked metal men.

"Yes, I do like. They are beautifully made," I commented, wandering around one of the statues and admiring the shapely sculptured ass of the statue. "These are incredibly well done," I continued. "I like the contours and definition of the bodies. Obviously it is the same model that has been used for each statue."

"You are right."

"I think this model has a beautiful body in every way," I continued, feeling the biceps and running my hands over the chest area of one of the statues.

"I show you more. Come, we go," said my guide, taking my arm and leading me away from the ten metal men.

"Where are we going now?" I asked, as we dodged traffic and pedestrians.

We walked for some time, again wandering along narrow alleys until we reached a secluded garden next to a very ordinary building. The garden was plain, without floral decorations, but situated close to a shrubbery, lay a smooth marble statue of a bald, naked person. I say person, because it was difficult to determine what sex the model was because of its obesity. The statue was of a reclining bald person, grossly overweight, with a stomach and chest area that seemed to roll into one, thereby making it difficult to determine whether the model had a bosom or whether it had over-sized pectorals. The rolls of stomach flooded downwards towards two equally fat thighs which were equaled in size to the stomach and because of their size eliminated the possibility of determining whether the model had a penis or not. Just as the rolls of excess fat seemed to move from the upper body, so it traveled down the legs to end in two over large ankles. The arms and hands resembled the legs and the neck was as thick as the bald head. Although the smooth carving showed a grotesque figure, it was attractive in its obscenity to look at. I started in absolute wonder at the work of the artist, but also felt for the person on whom the artist had modeled this statue.

"What you think?" asked my guide.

I burst out laughing; not at the workmanship but at the contrast from the metal men and now the marble woman.

"You find it funny?" asked my newly found friend.

"Oh no, not at all. In fact I think it beautifully created. It's just not what I would expect to see in a public park."

"You forget this is Bohemia. The artists here are unconventional in their creativity," he proudly announced to me.

He was right. I had never experienced art like he was showing me. They were both naked in the extreme, but I had found them sexy in an erotic way.

"These are done by the same artist," said my guide, offering me added information as there was no notice indicating the artist or the title of the pieces of art work.

I looked at the naked marble woman and stared in wonder how it had been sculptured out of a single block of marble, much like the ancient Greeks and Romans had done.

"You like to meet the artist?" asked my young guide.

"Yes please. Do you know the artist?"

Pavel smiled and nodded.

"Come I take you there."

He hurried ahead with me tagging along behind, trying to keep up with this athletic young man. Although it seemed that we had traveled for some time, I realized that we had gone very far; it was just that there were so many winding alley ways. We came to an old, yet elegantly decorated building and entered. We climbed three flights of stairs and came to an ornately carved front door. Instead of knocking, Pavel merely opened the door and entered. I hesitated and then followed him into a cleanly decorated home.

"Papa," shouted Pavel. "I have a guest here."

A middle-aged man, lean and good-looking entered the lounge area. Although he was lean, he still exuded strength and I could see from the firmness of his handshake that he was strong.

"Papa, this is David, a tourist to our beautiful city. I have been showing him your art."

This was the first time that I heard Paval mention anything about the artist being his father.

"Sir, I am wonder-struck by your art. I was unaware that it was your work and all I can say is that I found it not only well done, but, if I may say, sexually attractive."

Paval's father roared with laughter at my reference to the sexual attractiveness.

"I must ask; who were the models?"

"Paval and his mother."

"Oh!" was all I could say, as I suddenly had a flash of memory of what I had said to Pavel while we were standing next to the metal men.

"You seem surprised," said Pavel, grinning at me.

"Well, I was … uhm … they were … I didn't know… I liked them very much," I stammered.

As we stood there in the lounge, me flabbergasted, a large bald woman entered the room, dressed in a flowing caftan garment. Then I recognized the face of the bald, naked statue reclining in the park: it was Paval's mother. She greeted me warmly but soon left the room, leaving Pavel, his father and myself to discuss the sculptures.

"You seemed surprised that my models were my own family," said Paval's father.

"Well yes. And they didn't mind being sculptured in the nude; especially for the whole world to see?"

Both Paval and his father laughed heartily.

"We are not ashamed of the naked body; after all it is a thing of beauty. You yourself admired my work, didn't you?"

"Absolutely," I replied.

"Paval, I have an idea. Why don't you and your friend here pose for me and I shall create another work of art?"

"What did you have in mind, Papa?"

"Rodin's Kiss!"

Paval turned to me, smiled and agreed with his father.

"I think that would make a wonderfully controversial sculpture," Paval stated.

I must have had a slightly blank look on my face because both men, on seeing my expression laughed warmly.

"You seem surprised, young man," said Paval's father, scurrying out of the room to fetch a sketch pad. "Come to my studio," he shouted to us as he departed.

Paval and I made our way to another room which was the art room cum studio. All around the walls of the room were pencil sketches, small statues, including a miniature version of both statues of Paval and his mother.

In the center of the room, Paval's father had placed a rectangular block on which we were to sit.

"Take off your clothes," commanded Paval's father, "and Paval I want you seated there on the block, and Ian, I want you to sit on Paval's lap, but sideways on."

I watched with interest as Paval peeled off his clothes with gusto, revealing an immaculately formed young body. As he stood naked in the room, I saw the resemblance to the ten metal men. His defined physique was theirs, his broad shoulders were theirs, even down to his well-hung cock, and it was theirs. O became slightly aroused by the beauty I saw before me. Slowly I undressed, allowing my arousal to subside before I removed my briefs.

"Paval sit on the block. Now Ian, sit sideways on Paval's lap, but turn your upper body so that your face is looking into his and your lips are touching."

Paval sat and I positioned myself on his lap. I felt his sturdy legs supporting my naked ass, and also felt the slight firmness of his cock resting under me. I wrapped an arm around his neck and turned my upper body so that we were face-to-face. I stared into his smiling face and as I did so our mouths made contact.

"Right! Hold it like that," shouted his father, who busied himself sketching our position.

I closed my eyes as I thought about this muscular young man, holding me in his arms while his father walked around our naked bodies, sketching us. Holding our position was tiring, but very soon after we had sat down I felt Paval's cock begin to nudge my ass. I could feel his erection growing beneath me and this was turning me on. Soon I knew that my cock was fully erect and that his father could see this phenomenon, but he never said a word. Our mouths no longer rested casually lip-on-lip, but instead, I felt Paval's tongue force its way between my lips and enter my mouth. This in itself was a complete turn-on for me and I hastily reciprocated. His father sketched furiously from every perspective, while Paval and I allowed our hands to explore each other's body.

After what seemed eternity, Paval's father heaved a sigh and said, "That is me finished; now I will leave you two young men to finish also." He placed his sketch pad in a safe place, exited and closed the door behind him.

Paval and I broke our kiss for the first time and smiled at each other. I rose from my awkward position and turn to face him then I lowered myself onto his waiting cock, allowing him to slide effortlessly into my warm confines. As he rested, imbedded in me, I gently rose and fell on his length, while kissing him at the same time. From the block that we had been seated upon, we moved onto the floor where we rolled around while 'glued' to each other, our passion taking us all around the room until we were filled with each other's love.

Once our exhausted, sweaty bodies had returned to some form of normality, Paval asked if I would like to take a shower and clean up. I readily accepted and the two of us showered together, dressed and then he took me back to my hotel, where we started all over again.

A year later, and after constant e-mails and telephone calls between Paval and me, I was back in Prague. I had called Paval and told him of my arrival date, so he was at the airport to meet me, but instead of taking to his home to see his mother and father, he took me into the city first.

"Where are we going?" I enquired as the car sped along the main streets.

"I am taking you to Střelecký ostrov, an island in the middle of the Vltava River."

"What for," I asked as we continued speeding along the busy roads.

We came to the river, parked the car and walked across the bridge until we reached the island. We descended the step of the bridge and landed on the green turf of the island, then Paval led the way. Soon we came to an opening and Paval stopped. I looked at what was in front of us and stared in awe.

"Paval, that is beautiful," was all I could say, as I wandered around the work of art that stood among the trees. "Your father is fantastic. Oh my God!" I exclaimed and stopped in my tracks.

"You like?" asked Paval, obviously extremely proud of his father's work.

"He's even included our erections!"

"That is what I think is beautiful. Look how sturdy and smooth your long cock is and how tight your ass looks as I am about to enter you."

I blushed, but I had to acknowledge that as a piece of art, it was beautifully sculptured in every detail.

"You are now party of Bohemia, Ian; you are part of our family now," said Paval hugging me and kissing me in the tranquility of the parkland environment.

- SEX ON THE BEACH -

Ingredients:

½ a full Cranberry juice
½ a full Pineapple juice
1 oz Vodka
¾ oz Peach Schnapps

Directions:

Put in Vodka and Peach Schnapps and then fill remainder with half each of the juices. Stir in a highball glass.

SANDY BAY

Sandy Bay is, as its name suggests, a bay made up of a beautiful stretch of powdery, soft, white beach sand surrounded by large granite boulders providing shelter for the sun-worshiper from any prevailing winds. The beauty of Sandy Bay is that because of its secluded nature, many people strip off and tan in the nude; in fact it's become renowned as a nudist beach, although this is not entirely obligatory. An added feature of this beach is that it is seldom overcrowded with bodies absorbing the sun's rays and that is why I chose to spend the morning there.

I made myself comfortable between two large boulders, almost closing myself in a sort of sun trap, and stripped down to my Speedo. Although I was secluded, I chose not to join the few other people I'd seen, showing my 'wares' to the world. I placed my towel on the cool sand and lay down on my stomach, feeling the sun's rays warm my back and legs.

I lay there for some time, listening to the crash of waves on the adjacent rocks and feeling the warmth envelop my body. I was just beginning to doze off into a trance-like state when I heard a voice.

"Excuse me, but would you like me to put some oil on your back for you?"

I lifted my head from my prone position and turned behind me. The sun caught my eyes, temporarily blinding me. The area that I had chosen to lay my towel down had been deserted, so where did this voice come from?

"I'm sorry," I said, trying to make out who had spoken to me.

"I asked if you'd like me to rub some tanning oil on your back before you get burnt red," repeated the soft baritone voice.

My eyes focused and I blinked, not believing what I saw. My visitor had to be a bodybuilder, and if not, he must have been a regular gym bunny. The pecs were pumped, along with the biceps. The broad shoulders tapered down to what appeared to be a 30 inch waist and the abs resembled a sheet of corrugated iron. The legs were like two large oak tree trunks and the cropped blonde-haired man was wearing a pale blue silky Speedo. He stood on a granite rock, looking down at me. He stood astride on the rock for a moment almost like the statue to Colossus and then sprang down onto the cool sand alongside me. There was so much body to take in that I wasn't quite sure where to focus my attention, but the full package encased in Lycra did feature strongly. His package was so heavy and defined that I could clearly make out the long, thick stem attached to the bulbous, mushroom-shaped circumcised head – just what I liked.

Once I had taken in this vision and sorted out my painfully disoriented brain, I picked up the bottle of tanning oil and passed it to him, without moving from my towel.

"Thanks," I said, with a tone of surprised wonder in my voice.

Where had this god come from and why to me? Nobody had ever made an offer like this before, but I'm not one to reject an offer from a good-looking young man, and so was happy to accept.

I felt him position himself between my outspread legs, then felt the cold spray of oil across my shoulders, followed by the gentle touch of finger tips as my visitor began to massage the oil into my shoulder blades and upper arms. Although his touch was gentle, there was firmness in his hands. His hands moved across my shoulders and onto my biceps. I felt his hands slide over each bicep and instinctively I tensed them, allowing my visitor to massage them deeply. He repeated his strokes twice, ensuring that my arms were well-coated with suntan oil. His hands then covered my upper back and then made their slippery way down to my lower back. I felt his fingers move across the top of my Speedo and down the sides of my waist. An awakening was taking place in my crotch as his sensual touch sent erotic tingles through my body.

"Can I do the legs?" came the soft voice.

I was now well and truly in a trance-like state, so I merely groaned in a fashion as if to say, 'don't stop!'

The cool spray of suntan oil covered my left leg and then I felt my calf muscles being massaged.

My 'masseur' slowly made his way up my calf and thigh, his fingers sliding effortlessly on the inside of my leg until his finger tips reached the bottom of my Speedo. His hands massaged my upper thigh, moving his fingers along the inside of my leg until his finger tips nudged my balls, and then were gone. Three times his hands slid up and down my leg, nudging my balls each time he reached them.

I felt the cold spray on my right leg and the whole procedure was repeated. By this time I was fully erect and my cock was now pressing uncomfortably against my stomach. I raised my butt to adjust the lie of my cock and he must have noticed.

When he reached the upper thigh of my right leg, his fingers slid between my legs and, instead of nudging, he gently caressed my balls. I knew that as he did this, he would feel the hardness of the base of my cock, but neither of us spoke.

I once again heard the sound of the spray but felt nothing, then I realized he'd sprayed oil onto his hands because both oily hands rested on each upper thigh. Gingerly, his fingers edged under the Lycra material of my Speedo and I soon felt a firm touch on each ass cheek. His hands massaged my ass and I raised it slightly as if to acknowledge my liking of his movements. His hands slid into my crack and I felt his fingers slide, ever so lightly, over my entrance. He repeated this action a couple of times, driving me crazy and with each stroke I raised my ass hoping he'd make an entry.

I felt an oil-slick finger rub my waiting hole and then slide effortlessly into my warm confines. Once inside, I felt it exploring, then escaping. I sighed at my loss, but not for long. I felt two fingers slide in, while the fingers on the other hand massaged the area between my crack and my balls.

This man was an expert. I felt my cock oozing pre-cum as my hole twitched with each anticipated move his fingers made.

Suddenly everything stopped!

His fingers disappeared from the confines of my hole and I panicked, but before I could raise my head to see what was happening, I felt his hands on the waistband of my Speedo. He was pulling my Speedo down to my ankles to reveal my white ass. It was actually a pleasure to have my butt out in the open, getting some sun on it.

No sooner had he done this, but I heard him removing his Speedo. Once he'd removed his Speedo, his hands resumed their massaging action and I could feel how he was spreading my ass cheeks, then I felt the wetness of the tip of his tongue. He flicked his tongue tip in and out of my hole causing it to flutter and while he did this, I felt a hand slide under my balls in search of my hardened cock.

A slick hand found what it was searching for and I could feel how he oiled up my cock, his fingers sliding and massaging my cut cock-head.

As soon as he started this, my moans of pleasure started up audibly. Three fingers now replaced his tongue, but his other hand remained busily sliding with ease along my oil-slicked rock-hard stem.

My moans had now become groans and my butt was rising and falling more regularly as I rode his fingers and he worked my cock.

"Oh yes!" I gasped. "Fuck me, please!"

I felt him remove both hands and I heard the suntan oil spray go again then heard him slicking up his cock. He placed both hands on either side of my upper body then gently lowered himself across my back. I could feel his engorged cock rub against my ass cheeks. Then he began sliding slowly over my oil-slicked back. Each time he rubbed himself across my body, I could feel his cock poking at my ass crack in search of my hole. I began to writhe against him in an effort to help guide his cock into me.

At last I felt him at my entrance. Slowly he began to slide in. I could feel that he was big, as he stretched me in his effort to breach me. I pushed up and gasped as his large head broke through. He froze for a moment, and then sank deeper into me until his balls slapped against my slick ass. We lay there attached but not moving. In our moment of stillness, I could feel his cock throbbing inside of me. It was jerking so much that I wasn't sure whether he was coming.

Gently he raised himself from me, pulling his cock along the length of my chute until just the large head remained embedded, and then he sank slowly into me again.

This action continued for some time as his thick, slick cock produced a dizzying effect on me. With each movement, my prostate was rubbed, causing me to leak pre-cum profusely and creating a sensational feeling of euphoria.

After about five minutes of constant slow fucking, he held onto me and rolled us both onto our sides, without us losing connection. He put a hand between my legs and lifted one of them into the air, spreading my legs wide while he continued with his slow fuck.

His cock was obviously so thick that it felt like I had a cucumber in me, but the tightness was pleasing to both of us.

A breathy voice said, "Ride me. Ride my dick!"

I pushed back and in doing so, rolled him onto his back while I rolled with him. Now that I was on top of him, I sat up, getting full penetration, and then slowly and carefully, without loosing connection, I turned around on his cock until I faced him.

We both smiled as we saw each other properly for the first time. I rubbed my hands across his pumped up pecs, nipping his two protruding nubs. As I did this, so he plowed upwards into me. I leaned forward and licked each nipple in turn, chewing on them gently and feeling the effect in my ass. I felt the suntan oil spray cover my cock and then his hand began massaging my sand-encrusted cock. The small granules of sea sand being rubbed along my length created a teasingly erotic pleasure which was drawing me closer to flooding his chest and stomach with pent-up cum.

"Oh fuck me hard," I shouted, riding his thick cock as though I were riding a horse.

We were both sweating profusely from the intense action and the heat. His hand was working my cock and I was gritting my ass muscles so as to create a tight, strangulating hold on his massive weapon.

Our grunts and groans were now excessively amplified and I knew we were both about to please each other.

"Aaargh!" I cried as I felt my balls rise in my sac.

My body tensed as my cum rose from the depths of me and fired like a catapult across my 'masseur's' chest, hitting him on the chin.

"Fuck me!" I growled, riding his cock for all I was worth.

My ass gripped tightly around his cock as I rammed down, slapping my ass cheeks against his balls. I gyrated my ass, grinding against his pelvis as if trying to get his balls into my hole.

"Oh fuck!" he shouted, plowing my ass and getting red in the face. He held my waist and raised me slightly then pumped his thick cock into my tight, pulsating hole.

Our gasps, groans, cries and breathing were matched only by the vociferous slapping together of one body against another. My cock felt raw from the intense pumping it had received, but I knew it could take more, especially from someone like my 'masseur'.

As our breathing began to return to a sense of normality, I remained impaled on him, feeling his cock pulsate in my ass, which was now oozing some of his cum. I leant forward and our lips met, gently touching. Our tongues entered each other's mouth and we lay in the blazing sun, still attached.

As my mouth left his, I smiled and said, "Hi, I'm Gary."

"And I'm Brent," came the response.

"Well Brent, how would you like to come back to my hotel room to clean up and then we can start all over again?"

Brent smiled, gave an upwards thrust into my ass and replied, "I can't wait to attack that cute ass of yours again!"

- CARUSO -

Ingredients:

1½ oz Gin
1 oz Dry Vermouth
1 oz Green Crème de Menthe

Directions:

In a mixing glass half filled with ice, combine all of the ingredients. Stir well. Strain into a cocktail glass.

PULAU JADE

The tranquility surrounding me was broken by the sound of a *thud* on the white sand next to me. I lay on my back in the warm sunshine and opened my eyes. I didn't see anyone, but as I turned my head to one side, I noticed a coconut lying on the sand near my head. It had fallen from the tall palm tree that had been giving me a little shade before the sun had moved.

"That's a sign of good luck," a voice said from behind me.

I craned my neck and noticed a young man of about nineteen leaning against the trunk of the palm tree.

"Do you mean it was good luck that it missed me?" I enquired.

"Oh no," he laughed. "If it had hit you that would have been a sign of bad luck."

How right he was. I probably would have been knocked unconscious.

I flipped over onto my stomach so that I could get a better view of my wise young man. He was obviously a local with dark hair, pearly white teeth that gleamed when he smiled, was tall and slim but athletically muscular. This was evidenced by the fact that he wore only a pair of ragged shorts, which also revealed a pair of sturdy legs and as he was shirtless, a finely muscular upper torso with a ripped stomach revealing a six-pack. I liked what I saw.

To alleviate stretching my neck to look up at him, he came and sat alongside of me on the sand. I turned onto my side so that we were now face-to-face.

"You obviously live here," I stated, smiling at my new friend.

"Yes. I live in the village on the other side of the mountain. My family is made up of fishermen and I help out when I'm needed," he replied in near perfect English.

I wondered if his muscularity was as a result of having to row boats out to sea in order to fish.

"Have you been here long?" asked my visitor.

"Do you mean here at the beach or on the island?"

"The island," he answered.

"Three days and I have another week to go before I return home," I replied.

"Have you been around Pulau Jade yet?" he enquired.

I shook my head and said that I was looking forward to seeing as much as possible of his island before I left.

"Would you like me to show you around?"

Although I had found all the inhabitants that I had met on the island to be friendly, no one had offered to show me their island. I looked deeply into his face and decided that going around the island with a local, like the one offering his services, would be far more beneficial than doing it by myself, because he would know where all the hidden spots were; the type that the tourists don't get to.

"I would like that very much," I said, stretching out a hand to shake his. "Gary is my name."

"You can call me Manu."

We shook hands and I noticed how firm his grip was and how his biceps tensed as he gripped my hand. A warm feeling rushed through my body and I felt a gentle tingling in my groin as a result of his touch. Maybe the falling coconut was going to be good luck for me.

"Why is this island called Pulau Jade?" I enquired.

"Just look over there," he answered, pointing to the hillside that surrounded the beach. "What do you see?"

"Jungle!"

"Exactly. There is tropical jungle everywhere except where hotels have been built and near the beach areas, so if you look at the island everything seems green like the color jade."

When I heard his answer, I thought that having asked him that question was very stupid of me because once I realized the answer, it was so logical. Any rate, we lay chatting for quite some time until I became unbearably hot.

"I think I need to cool off with a swim. Are you going to join me?"

Without waiting for a reply, I scurried over the burning, white sand and headed into the crystal clear aqua-marine sea with its gently lapping waves. I dived under the water and when I surfaced I noticed that Manu had also entered the water. We splashed like two small children, frolicking in the liquid coolness. Once I had cooled down sufficiently, I headed back to my towel and lay on my back watching Manu still enjoying himself in the water. Eventually he emerged from the sea and headed back to where I was. As I watched him walk, I could see how his wet shorts clung to his body, revealing the outline of his long, thick cock, which hung down the left leg of his shorts. The sight was breathtaking and I could feel an arousal in my Speedo as I watched him near me. I slid to the edge of my towel so that he could share part of it with me, rather than sitting on the hot sand.

"You can sit here," I said, patting the towel next to me, "then you won't get burnt on the sand."

Manu gladly accepted the invitation to share the towel as the sand had become unbearably hot to the touch. Because of our close proximity, it was inevitable that our bodies would touch, and the more we touched, the more aroused I became. The bulge in my Speedo was growing immensely and I knew that Manu could see this, but he never moved away nor did he say anything about it. His left arm rubbed against my right side and I enjoyed his touch. I tried to focus on anything else in the hopes that I would begin to lose my hard-on, but without avail. I decided that there was nothing I could do about my erection except let it take on a life of its own.

"You like this island?" asked Manu, making eye contact with me.

"Very much. I saw some beautiful photos in the travel brochure and that's why I chose to come here."

"You like the people here too?"

"Absolutely!" Not that I had met many locals other than the staff at the nearby hotel, but those that I had met seemed very friendly.

For a moment there was a deathly quietude and nobody spoke, but we remained looking at each other. It was one of those awkward moments we often have when we meet a person for the first time. After what seemed an eternity, Manu spoke.

"You have a nice body," said Manu, glancing over my torso.

"Thank you Manu, but so have you."

He smiled at the compliment and turned on his side so as to lean on an elbow and look at me.

"You are big," he said, his eyes twinkling as he said it.

I became a little embarrassed but this was compounded as I looked down at his crotch to see if there had been any changes taking place there, but his long cock still lay outlined flaccidly under his shorts. My own cock throbbed once or twice in my Speedo and its complete outline was very evident: my cock's bulbous head poked close to the waist band of my Speedo, as though it were trying to escape and find daylight. Although my bathing costume had dried after the swim, a small wet patch emerged on my sky-blue Speedo where the tip of my cock was situated. Manu noticed this and grinned at me, but never commented on it.

The beach was deserted, so anything could have happened between the two of us, but I wasn't about to make the first move. Although I felt that I desperately wanted Manu to touch my throbbing cock, I wasn't sure of their island customs or whether he was into having man-sex. I was also unsure how a nineteen-year-old young man might perceive any advances I might make towards him, so I let things be and tried to get him out of my mind, which was proving very difficult.

"I think I've had enough sun for one day," I said rising from the towel, and adjusting the lie of my cock in my Speedo. "I think I'll make my way back to the hotel."

"Which hotel are you staying at?"

"The Lagoon Resort."

"Are you in one of those huts built over the sea?"

I smiled and nodded. "The one right on the very end of the water villas."

"It must be wonderful sleeping above the water and knowing that in the morning you can go down your stairs and straight into the sea."

"It is actually."

"Will I see you again, Gary?" asked Manu.

It was the first time that he had used my name since our meeting, so I took it to mean that he might just be interested in me, but it could also be wishful thinking on my part.

I said my farewells and made my way to my 'hut' as Manu had called it. In fact it was a luxurious villa built on stilts over the sea. At night as one lay in bed, one could hear the gentle lapping of the water against the steps that led up to a private patio, and if a breeze blew, the scents from the tropical gardens and jungle wafted out over the sea and into the villa. The main part of the hotel was situated on the mainland, surrounded by verdant jungle and tropical foliage while most of the accommodation was over the sea, surrounded by refreshingly clear seas.

I made my way along the boarded walkway, which led from the main hotel out to the villas perched over the sea. On entering my villa, I stripped off my Speedo and grasped my balls to give them a gentle squeeze as though to waken them up and bring me to an arousal again. I wandered out onto the patio in my naked state and sat dangling my legs over the edge of the patio. The water glistened and sparkled in the bright sunshine, while a couple of small fish darted hither and thither. I then wandered back indoors and went to lie down on my bed. It was wonderfully cool inside of the villa, with its ceiling fan gently brushing the air. With the coolness of the interior and the softly lapping waters against my outside stairs, I soon dozed off to sleep.

On awakening, my cock was fully erect and I lay on my back playing with myself, slowly stroking my cock and thinking of Manu, wondering what he would look like completely naked.

After an evening meal, I returned to my villa and settled down for a good night's rest. A full moon shone boldly on the calm sea, illuminating the surrounding areas. I ventured down my stairs and dropped my naked body gently into the cool waters. I swam a little way from my villa towards one of the others and then headed back. I climbed from the sea, dripping water as I made my way back up to my patio but once inside, I dried myself and went to lie on the bed in the moonlight. As I lay there I heard a distant splashing of someone also having a moonlight swim.

As I lay in the moonlit room, a silhouette appeared at the sliding door of the bedroom, which led onto the patio. I could see the muscular outline with the well-developed arms and legs, and immediately my heart skipped a beat. I lay waiting in anticipation as the silhouette neared the side of my bed.

"Gary, are you awake?" whispered a voice.

I pretended to be asleep.

I felt the wet body get onto the bed and sidle up next to me; then I felt a cool hand slide between my legs and nudge my balls. I adjusted my position allowing my visitor free access to my crotch. His hand wandered over my tight balls and made its way to the base of my hard cock. Slowly his fingers trailed up along my shaft until they reached the tip where they flicked my cock-head. I groaned as I felt this excitingly, invigorating pleasure.

The visitor adjusted his position on the bed and lowered his head to meet my throbbing cock. I felt the tip of his tongue encircle my circumcised head, then felt his warm mouth encompass my length and sink down to my shaft's base. He held his position while I savored the sensation and thrust upwards.

"Aargh, Manu, that feels great," I groaned, trying desperately to get my cock deeper down his throat.

I felt for his groin and to my joy was greeted by his thick, long cock, erect and ready for action. I wriggled to maneuver myself so that I could reciprocate by taking his thick pole down my throat and treat him in much the same way that he was treating me. As our mouths worked on each other, so our hands wandered over the other's body. I felt a finger run down my ass crack, in search of my pulsating entry. As Manu's fingers touched my asshole, it clamped shut, causing his fingers to attempt to pry it open. It didn't take much effort to open me up, as I was delirious with desire for this virile nineteen-year-old islander to treat me in the way that I envisaged the islanders to treat their guests.

His mouth left my cock and he lifted my hips so as to get easier access to my ass. I felt his rough tongue graze my asshole and then felt as he slipped the tip of his tongue into my opening. My asshole quivered as he dug deeply with his tongue, inserting it as far as he could into me, while his hand worked along my length, which was beginning to ooze a stream of shiny pre-cum.

"Will you fuck me, Manu?" I pleaded, but he seemed to be too preoccupied with his task at hand and continued rimming me.

I'm sure that he knew that he was driving me crazy, because the more I pleaded with him; the more he chose to ignore my pleas. For such a young man, I was well aware how experienced he was at pleasing me sexually.

"Do you have a condom?" he asked.

I stretched across to the side table next to the bed and got one as well as some KY, which I always carried with me.

When he felt I was ready, he handed me the condom and told me to unwrap it on his cock. I tore open the wrapper, and, using my mouth, I slowly unrolled it down his length. Once my chin rubbed up against his balls, I released my grip and raised myself until I was kneeling above Manu's manhood. He lay on his back and watched in the moonlight as I slowly lowered myself over his cock. I held his thick shaft and guided it towards my waiting asshole. Slowly and gently, I pushed down, gradually impaling myself on his weapon. I felt an initial sharp pain as his girth expanded my opening, but I was determined to take him. I sank lower and lower, my eyes fixed on Manu's and we both held our breaths as I sank. The pain turned to absolute pleasure and as I felt his cock-head pass through my sphincter, I relaxed and allowed him total control. I sighed as my ass hit his pelvis and he gave a little upward thrust as if to welcome me onto his extended pole.

My excitement was beyond explanation, but I wasn't about to let Manu know that I could stay like this for the entire night. I began riding his cock with gusto, enjoying each thrust that he offered, while at the same time, I leant forward to place my mouth over his protruding nipples. Gently I chewed on them then licked them, watching in the moonlight as he thrust not only his cock into me, but also thrust his chest up towards my mouth, encouraging me to take his nipples.

After riding Manu's cock for what seemed like an eternity, he rolled me onto my side without losing any contact and continued impaling me. Now our mouths sought each other's and our tongues fought to control the other's mouth. Our hands were all over each other and our bodies thrashed like two sharks fighting over a piece of meat.

He rolled me onto my back, lifted my legs high above my head and forced himself deeper into my pulsating asshole. I tried to pull him deeper into me, but already his cock was embedded to its full length.

Our breathing became more intense and hurried. Our thrusts were more frantic and each of us reached closer and closer to our moment of ecstasy where even the crashing oceans would not drown out our cries of happiness and lust.

I gasped as a thick wad of white juice fired from my throbbing cock, hitting me across the chest; then a second was fired, followed quickly by a third. My ass muscles clamped tightly around Manu's pounding cock and I felt his passion as he let loose into me. His grunts and cries as he fired load after load of seed into me must have awoken any mermaid or merman who might have been dreaming in the bottom of the oceans.

Our passion complete, Manu and I lay entwined in each other's arms, allowing our breathing to return to some form of normality. Our lips touched and we caressed each other, while still remaining connected.

The peacefulness of the night and the gentle lapping of the water beneath my room overcame us and soon we were asleep in each other's arms, my cock slightly flaccid, while Manu's was still hard, erect and embedded in me.

During the night, or what seemed to be the early hours of the morning, I heard a splash from outside and when I awoke, feeling like a prince, I noticed that Manu had left, but next to the bed was a hastily scribbled note telling me that the following day he was going to take me to his village on the other side of the mountain.

The following day arrived and a message was sent to my villa informing that there was someone to see me at reception. I dressed and made my way to meet my visitor. Manu was standing waiting for me. He looked so tall and majestic, so mature and beautiful; his dark hair set off against his tanned face with its refined features and the white shorts and t-shirt that he wore contrasted with his tanned body. I wanted to hug and kiss him, but obviously I would not do so in front of the hotel staff.

"Where are we going today?" I asked, wanting to touch him as I spoke.

"We're going to trek through the jungle to my village on the other side of the mountain as I promised."

The thought of mountaineering was a daunting task for me, but Manu assured me that there'd be no such thing and that the path he had chosen was very easy to negotiate.

We set off, me following close behind him as we entered the tropical jungle which bordered the main buildings of the hotel. As he led the way, I watched with fascination as his well-developed thighs moved confidently and with them, his ass. My focus remained fixed on his ass encased in his tight white shorts. Each mound moved hypnotically and soon I was being mesmerized by his ass movement.

The route was easy going as he had promised and it was refreshingly shady, but very humid under the canopy of the jungle. I had stripped off my shirt to try to remain cool, but I could still feel rivulets of sweat trickling down my neck and back. At one stage, I became so mesmerized by Manu's tight ass that I had to touch him. My hands went instinctively to the two firm mounds of flesh and I grabbed. He stopped in his tracks and turned to face me.

"What was that for?" he asked, laughing.

"I'm sorry. I just had to do that. Your ass is so sexy in those tight shorts that I just had to have a feel of it."

Manu smiled again, but this time with a wicked twinkle in his eye.

"You like my ass, Gary?" he coyly asked.

Staring deeply into his eyes, I replied, "Yes Manu, very much."

"You want?" he asked, patting his tight ass.

I licked my lips and smiled. "I want!"

Without any hesitation, Manu made a detour from the path we were traveling along and I followed. We cut through some thick foliage until we emerged into a small opening. He threw down his backpack that he'd been carrying and took off his shirt and threw that onto the ground. He then took my shirt from me and threw that down next to his, and then he lay down on our shirts. I stared admiringly down at this young man with his taut stomach muscles, his muscular arms tucked under his head and his legs spread apart. He was tempting me and I wasn't about to let that wonderful package that he had in his shorts go to waste. I knelt down between his legs and began to work on his ever growing package. His cock was swelling and growing longer, but so was mine. I took hold of the waistband of his shorts and in one movement had jerked them to his ankles. His hardened cock bounced up into the air, waiting to be moistened. My mouth was waiting to do just that and I decided that after the night spent together, it was now my turn to give Manu as much pleasure as he had given me.

While wild birds twittered in the trees above us and as the tranquility of the jungle enveloped us, so I enveloped Manu, sliding my throbbing cock-head into his waiting entrance. At no stage did Manu cry out in any pain, not that I was small in that area, but I had left the KY back at the hotel so we had no lubrication, other than sweat. I felt his tightness and knew that he had not often given himself to other men like this.

"Oh fuck, you're so tight," I sighed as I sank into him.

The tightness of his ass and the closeness of his heaving body were drawing me closer to coming, so I warned him.

He smiled when he heard me and answered, "I want you to fuck me like I did to you. I want you to enjoy me as I enjoyed you."

On hearing this, I gave myself over to utter lust and began frantically pounding his ass. The more and harder I pounded, the more Manu thrust onto my cock, allowing me to go deeper and deeper into him. The sweat was pouring from both of us; our bodies sliding with each touch from the heat and moisture.

Our moment of pleasure reached its climax at the same time. I gasped, cried out and tensed as I fired my first shot. As I tensed so Manu thrust rapidly on my cock, milking it dry as he did so, but at the same time, firing his own load onto his chest and arms. Once I was exhausted of all cum, I flopped forward onto Manu's chest and rubbed his warm cum with my face. I lathered his chest with it, kissing his body as I did so. I focused on his nipples and nibbled them which made him thrust his still hard cock into my stomach. I reciprocated by giving a couple of deep thrusts into his luxuriously warm ass.

"You wanted my ass, didn't you?"

"I sure did and it was magic. I don't think I've had the pleasure of making love to such a tight ass before. You were fantastic, Manu!"

Manu smiled up and me and pulled me closer to him, kissing me as he did so.

"We can stay here for the rest of the day if you like, or we can continue with our journey," he said, that wicked smile emerging on his face.

What temptation!

All I can say is that I never got to see his village, but I certainly got to know Manu better and what the inside of his tropical jungle resembled.

- ADONIS -

Ingredients:

1½ oz Dry Sherry
¾ oz Sweet Vermouth
1 dash Orange bitters

Directions:

Stir all the ingredients with ice. Strain the contents into a cocktail glass and serve.

REFLECTIONS
OF A BALD PHALLUS

I woke up this morning thinking it was just another day, just another of those mundane days, but when Brad gave me a squeeze and a shake to wake me up properly, I suddenly remembered today was my birthday. No, let me rephrase that, it was our birthday. Today both Brad and I turned twenty-six and Brad had invited a couple of friends round for dinner that evening. So this was not going to be one of those unexciting, humdrum days.

Brad and I had been together from birth and had stayed attached to each other through thick and thin, hard and soft times, ups and downs, and I had never let him down, although there were times that I thought he was letting me down. But, before I go any further, let me introduce myself to you.

Twenty-six years ago I came into this world, much like Brad had, and since that time, I had answered to the name of *Fred*. It wasn't the sort of name I would have given myself, but Brad decided that I was a Fred; whatever a Fred looked like. I remember at an early age undergoing a major 'haircut' which resulted in me becoming bald, so to speak, and I have remained like that all my life. As Brad grew, so did I; when Brad exercised, which was quite often, so did I. When Brad slept, I also slept, but quite often I'd be up earlier than him. In most cases if I was up early, it wouldn't be long before Brad would be awake as well, and then we'd play together, which was fun for both of us.

I think growing up was an exciting time for Brad; but not necessarily for me. We often did all sorts of things together, but sometimes I didn't feel like cooperating with him, and I'd go back to sleep; I think much to his loathing.

I noticed that when Brad turned sixteen or thereabouts, he began abusing me. It had never been like this before, but I knew that it was not done with malice; however, sometimes I did think his behavior went a little too far. Sure, I can hear you saying that you would have laid charges against him for physical abuse, but because we're so close to each other, I never had the heart to do it, instead, I put up with it.

By the time I turned eighteen I had grown substantially bigger and had matured a great deal more. I was stronger, taller and a lot more developed. I was no longer the skinny thing that I was when I was much younger; instead I had put on weight and had filled out. I know that Brad thought I looked better and was often proud to show me off to some of his friends, which made me feel pleased.

I remembered the first time that Brad introduced me to one of his friends, and I must say that he's had many friends whom I've met. We had gone to a party one evening, and after having a few drinks, Brad started to talk to a young man who looked about eighteen-years old. After about fifteen minutes of deep conversation, the three of us made our way to the toilet. You know, a man has to relieve himself regularly when he's been drinking! We stood at the urinal and it was here that Brad introduced me to his friend properly. I must say his friend was extremely friendly towards me because before I could do much, he was kissing me. Oh, his mouth was all over me, licking and kissing, while Brad stood by and watched. I noticed how Brad's friend was fascinated by my bald head and spent most of his time kissing it. Eventually I felt that I had had enough so I showed him by spitting at him. I know that wasn't very polite of me to do that, but I had no other way of saying 'enough!' Brad didn't seem angry that I had done this. In fact the three of us went back to the party and carried on drinking as though nothing had happened.

After that night, I met many more friends of Brad's, both at his home or at parties. You must remember that Brad and I lived together, so wherever he went, I did likewise. No, I wasn't his alter ego as you might think, we were just very close to each other; in fact I was like a part of him. Brad liked me and I liked him. Although the abuse of his early years continued, it didn't worry me anymore as I'd grown stronger and there were times when I actually enjoyed it. Now I know you're going to say, 'hey, you're kinky', but then maybe I am, but that doesn't mean that Brad wasn't also kinky sometimes.

When Brad and I turned twenty-one, we had a massive party. He invited about forty people to come and celebrate our birthday, mostly his friends, but then his friends were my friends, so we were both happy to see them all.

The party was a roaring success and everyone was having a wonderful time. As the night progressed, so people started leaving to go home, but there still remained a few loyal friends who weren't in the mood to stop partying. By two in the morning, almost all had left except for Brad, Jonathan, Mike and me. The group sat chatting and then Brad made a suggestion that Jonathan and Mike stay the night as they'd already had a bit too much to drink and it wouldn't be safe for them to drive home in their current state. The arrangement was agreed upon and the four of us climbed into Brad's big double bed.

Brad and I lay in the middle with Jonathan and Mike on either side. Soon I felt a hand touch me and I became aroused. While the hand was touching me, I heard Brad groaning with pleasure, and then I felt someone kissing my head. This felt good and I hoped that Brad was also being treated royally. I recognized Jonathan's face as it neared me and I realized that it was he who was kissing me. Ooh, he had a lovely soft mouth; tender lips and a long, silky tongue that ventured in all directions around me. I had, in the meantime become extremely excited and I could feel that Brad wanted to do something more than just lie next to these two men.

The bed sheets got flung from the bed and Brad lay on his back with his legs hoisted high in the air while Mike aimed his thick shaft at Brad's pulsating pucker. Mike's cock sank slowly into the depths of Brad's warm ass and at the same time, Jonathan proceeded to start sucking on my head. It was the most extraordinary sensation and I knew that both Brad and I were enjoying the treatment that we were getting.

I listened to the grunts that Brad and Mike were making as Mike pummeled into Brad's tight ass and this was turning me on. I found Jonathan's mouth delectable and wanted more. A cry echoed around the room and I felt Brad jolt as he and I fired our combined load. Jonathan's mouth worked ferociously to take down all that was sent his way. I was impressed by his swallowing ability; as a matter of fact he never let any spill – this boy liked a lot! When Mike had emptied his load into Brad, both Brad and Mike began to work on Jonathan, bringing him to his climax. As Jonathan shot, so I felt a warm stream of young cum, splatter on me, then another stream until I was coated in a warm, sticky layer, which Mike then proceeded to lick off of me. Oh, what a night!

I remember another night when Brad decided to go the gym after work, so I went along for the ride. The place wasn't very busy, but that didn't stop Brad from doing some pseudo exercising, as I like to call it, followed by a steam bath and a shower. The exercise I didn't enjoy, but the steam bath and shower were the parts I liked.

After sweating a little on the weights machine, Brad and I headed off to the steam room, which was empty. We sat in the dark, warmth of the room, surrounded by volumes of steam which made us sweat. Brad stretched out his muscular legs and closed his eyes. I lay nonchalantly enjoying the sweat trickling down me. Suddenly the steam room door opened and a silhouette entered and sat on the tiled ledge where we were.

"Hi," said Brad, greeting the visitor.

"Hi there," responded the deep masculine voice. "You been training?"

"Yep," replied Brad, "and you?"

"Same," came the monosyllabic reply.

Silence reigned between the speakers.

"By the way, I'm Brad."

"Hi, and I'm Gary," replied the visitor.

I watched as the visitor, after a while, slid surreptitiously closer to where Brad was seated. Brad had his eyes open now and was also watching. Gary's left leg nudged Brad's right leg and the two seemed to remain glued together. The steam continued to hiss and the sweat continued to stream down us.

A little pressure was applied to Brad's leg by Gary, so I decided to get up and see what was happening. I began to raise my bald head in the steam as though looking around. Instinctively, Brad placed a hand on my head and rubbed it gently, as if to tell me not to be inquisitive. It actually felt rather good, as the steam had made my head slippery. He stroked my head much like one would stroke a cat, the only difference being that I wasn't about to get my claws into anyone. Every time he pushed down on me, I would spring back up to look around to see what was happening. Gary watched with interest as Brad stroked me.

Soon I felt another hand on my bald head. This was fun! Gary took to stroking me while Brad's hand moved across to the visitor and got busy there. Gary's hand was not as smooth as Brad's; he was probably a builder or handyman, with such rough hands, but it didn't worry me, in fact, it added pleasure. Brad pleasured Gary while he pleasured me. I watched as their mouths found each other and I heard their sucking of lips as they kissed, then Gary bent down to me and did likewise to me. I knew that Brad was happy that I was being treated well, because his moans reverberated around the steam room.

Just as soon as it started, so the kissing of my head ended. What was happening I wondered? Brad got up and took me with him, but where to? Then I saw.

Gary had lain down on the tiled ledge on which we had been sitting and Brad had positioned himself between Gary's strong legs. Brad held me tightly and moved closer to Gary. As we neared him, I caught the seductive musk odor coming from Gary. A smidgeon of light was coming through the glass door to the steam room and I noticed a small pink opening that was winking at me, as though trying to attract my attention. As I neared the opening and touched it, it slammed closed, but Brad was persistent that I should enter there.

Holding onto me tightly, Brad crept closer to Gary, taking me with him. Once more I spied the opening. It looked inviting and mysterious. I wanted to go in, but Gary seemed to be preventing me. Brad was not the type of person to mess about, so he decided for me. He pushed forward and I broke through the opening. A warm feeling overcame me and as I entered, I felt the door slam shut, but I was in. It was cozy inside this magical cave. The walls were close to me and I slid slowly into the unknown. Once I was deep inside this long tunnel, I actually jumped for joy at the pleasure the tight walls were creating for me. I felt myself begin to slide back and forth, and with each movement, I felt Gary tighten his grip on the passage along which I traveled.

I nudged something and as I did so, even though I was embedded in this dark tunnel, I heard Gary gasp and groan, much like I had heard Brad do before. I kept nudging this mound and each time I did so, I realized that Gary was growing more and more frantic with his actions. The opening through which I had entered had clamped very tightly around me and my slipping and sliding had become intensified. I was speeding up and down and I knew that this fast action was fun for me and Brad, and hopefully for Gary.

I continued to pound this nut-shaped object until I heard a loud growl from the outside and a strangulation-type grip on me. I thought I was going to have the life squeezed out of me, but I still managed to continue sliding back and forth. It was hot in the tunnel and with the sweat, my slipping and sliding allowed me to venture deeper into the tunnel. Oh wow! This was a rollercoaster ride of total ecstasy! I plummeted into the depths and then raced up to the entrance, only to dive deep into the dark unknown again. This backward and forward motion was speeding up and with it I felt a pleasure I had never felt in my life before. Suddenly I felt something deep inside of me, rising. As this 'something' rose, so a feeling of excitement came with it. I began to bounce and throb with joy and as it did so, the sweat in the dark tunnel became mingled with a salty-sweet mix of joy and pleasure. My head became covered in this fabulous mixture and still I continued slipping and sliding, diving deep down and then heading for the surface, but without breaking free. I could hear both Brad and Gary making pleasurable sounds in the steam room, but still I continued to blast into the tunnel. Finally things slowed down and I soon felt myself come to rest. I twitched and shuddered a couple of times as a few drops of sweat fell from my bald head, then I felt myself being slowly drawn upwards. As I reached the entrance, the door opened and the heat of the steam hit me. Both Brad and Gary were clutching each other, their lips sealed together, and as I lay there catching my breath, I rubbed up against my new found friend, who was just as sticky as I was.

"Hi there," I gasped, exhaustedly.

"Hi," came an equally exhausted voice. "What's your name?"

"*Fred*! What's yours?" I asked.

"*Willy*," he replied.

Willy looked very much like me – he was also bald, but was much fatter than me, although I thought I was taller than him.

"Nice to meet you. Do you think we'll see each other again?"

"I hope so. How was your journey?"

"I've never had one like that before, but it was fantastic. I could do it again," I said, dripping more sweat.

"I'm not into rollercoaster rides; I prefer just to be abused," *Willy* replied.

As I lay next to *Willy*, touching each other, I could feel both of us getting excited again.

"What's happening to us, *Willy*?"

"I think you might be going for another rollercoaster ride, *Fred*!"

***

As it was our twenty-sixth birthday, Brad had invited two friends around for dinner at the apartment; his recently newly acquired friend from the steam room at the gym, Gary, and a work friend named James. I think his intention was that the two friends might stay the night, but this decision was completely out of my hands.

The evening progressed well with everyone chatting and drinking merrily, and then at about eleven in the evening, Brad suggested that the friends stay the night. This was the first time that Gary and James had met each other, but both agreed to stay. I was very happy because it meant I would get to see *Willy* again.

"Why don't we hit the sack," suggested Brad, at about midnight.

"Where are we all sleeping?" asked James, waiting to see what plans Brad might have.

"We'll all fit onto the double bed, if that's OK with you guys?" said Brad, rising and heading towards the bedroom.

Gary and James followed.

In the room, everyone stripped off and climbed into bed, with Brad and me in the middle once more. I lay under the duvet and looked at *Willy* to my left, who seemed to be dozing. To my right I noticed that our other visitor was up and awake and looking to see what was happening.

"What's your name?" I whispered to the visitor on my right.

"What do you mean, 'what's my name'?"

"Well, haven't you got a name? That's *Willy* over there and I'm *Fred*."

The visitor looked blankly at me.

"I don't know what you mean."

"Well what does James call you?"

"He just calls me *Dick*."

"Oh all right, *Dick*, what do you like doing?"

"Anything, but I like a lot."

"Is that why you're already up and about?" I asked.

"I suppose you could say that. James likes me to be alert all the time."

"Even when you're not in bed?" I enquired.

"Sure, most of the time."

"But that must be quite tiring for you."

"It is sometimes, but then when I've had enough of standing around, I just go to sleep."

Just then James adjusted the way he was lying in the bed and I found myself face-to-face with *Dick*. I looked at him with interest because he wasn't bald like I and *Willie* were.

"You look different," I said, beginning to rise up to get a better look.

"I know, but I wish I looked like you, I think being bald is so sexy."

"That hat that you've got on your head, does it come off?"

"No, but I can roll it back if I want to, then I look a little like you."

"Can you show me?"

I watched with fascination as his hat slowly began to slide back to reveal a mushroom-shaped head like mine.

"That's fascinating," I said, as he drew closer to me.

As we lay side-by-side, I could see that *Dick* was bigger than me so I had to look up to him a bit.

Very soon both *Dick* and I were up close, face-to-face, rubbing against each other, while *Willy*, on the other side, was only now beginning to wake up. I saw Brad's hand go and wrap itself around *Dick* and start stroking him like he sometimes stroked me.

"Does that feel good?" I asked.

"Hm!" exclaimed *Dick*. "Your friend sure knows how to do things nicely."

By now *Willy* was wide awake and was trying to make contact with *Dick* and me, but was not having any luck. Suddenly the duvet flew off the bed and Gary's face appeared where *Dick* and I were lying. Gary took hold of both of us and began licking our heads, then he tried to swallow both of us together, but we were too big to both fit into his mouth. However, it didn't stop Gary from lathering us up, which we both enjoyed immensely.

I could see that some juice was beginning to come from the tip of *Dick*, which Gary hastily licked up.

James and Brad were entwined in each other's arms, kissing while Gary pleasured both of them. This continued for some time until James lay on his back and told Gary to sit on him and face him. I could see that Brad was a little surprised by this move, but didn't object.

Gary rose above James' groin and slowly lowered himself allowing *Dick* to slide effortlessly into the warm tunnel that I had hoped to visit once more. At first I was somewhat disappointed, but I soon realized what the plan was. *Willy* was jumping for joy as Gary began to ride on *Dick* and James began to thrust upwards.

"Slide in Brad," I heard James say, groaning as he said it.

Brad took hold of me and he aimed me at the beautifully pink entrance that I had enjoyed visiting previously, but I was concerned because the doorway was already filled with *Dick*.

Brad pushed me slowly forward and I slid along *Dick*. Our friction and warmth generated a feeling of ecstasy in me. I had found Gary's tunnel tight the first time I had ventured there, but it was even tighter now that both *Dick* and I were invading. I heard Gary cry out in pain as I slowly entered. *Dick* came to the opening to meet me and as soon as I had got through the opening and into the tunnel, we slipped down the warm confines together. I could feel *Dick*'s hat had been pulled back and was rubbing up against my bald head. This intense feeling was making me excited and little droplets of love juice oozed from my head and lubricated *Dick*. Together *Dick* and I began to slide like adjoining bodies, while Brad and James exerted more and more pressure on Gary's opening.

Gary no longer cried in pain, but rather in pleasure as the two men caressed his body and sank deeper and deeper into his warm interior. *Dick* and I were wet with sweat and the love juice that we were sharing between us, and with each thrust that James and Brad made, both of us found his nut-shaped mound and pounded it.

"Oh *Dick*," I gasped, "This is the best feeling that I have ever experienced. It's so tight in here and the feeling of you rubbing alongside of me is creating something unusual in me. I think I'm going to explode."

"*Fred*, if you've never experienced this before, doing it with a friend, you will again. I've been in this position many times and I really enjoy it, so does James."

Dick and I slid and slipped our way up and down the tunnel, bouncing and bobbing with excitement as we did so. It was great to have a friend with me on this rollercoaster ride, instead of doing it alone.

Brad and James' breathing was becoming more frantic and so were their thrusts, so much so that *Dick* and I were not in synchronicity any more, but rather it was like every man for himself.

"Oh Fuck!" exclaimed Brad. "I'm gonna come!"

"So am I," groaned James.

Both men increased their speed and both cried out together.

Dick shot a creamy white wad that landed on me, creating a fine lubrication for both of us. Soon more shots were being fired from both of us and as we excitedly slid in our warm tunnel, throbbing and shooting our loads, we became covered in love juice.

"This is a wonderful feeling," I sighed as *Dick* and I once again worked in unison. "I wonder how *Willy* is feeling."

"I would imagine he's ready to join us," replied *Dick*.

Brad's hand made contact with *Willy* and no sooner had he done that, than *Willy* fired his load onto James' chest.

As *Willy* fired so *Dick* and I felt the tunnel suddenly tighten around us.

"Ooh, this feels good," I cried as the tightness forced *Dick* and me closer together.

We clung to each other as the mixture of love juice continued to allow us to slide effortlessly.

With the three men beginning to revert to a form of normal breathing, I felt *Dick* beginning to move towards the entrance.

"Are you going so soon?" I asked.

"Looks like it."

"I'd like to stay a little longer," I replied, as I felt the slick *Dick* slide along me and exit.

I was alone in the warm, sticky tunnel, but I had enjoyed myself so much, I had stayed excited and had no intention of settling down.

Brad gave a couple of gentle thrusts into Gary and the two men remained attached to each other. This is what I liked. I was happy and didn't want to leave my warm burrow and I hoped that Brad would feel the same way.

During the rest of the night, I was constantly waking up and twice that night I had the joy of visiting the magical tunnel, but unfortunately, both times on my own; however, I know that *Dick* encountered a wonderful journey that night by exploring a different tunnel, that of Brad's, because in the early hours of the following morning both *Dick* and I were up and awake and we shared stories of the night's adventures as we rubbed up against each other.

As the years have rolled by, both Brad and I have made many friends and together we've spent many happy hours pleasuring each other, but Brad knows now what I like best – to go searching in warm, secluded tunnels for nut-shaped mounds that will bring absolute pleasure to Brad, me and his friends.

- FLORIDA -

Ingredients:

½ oz Gin
1½ tsp Kirschwasser
1½ tsp Triple sec
1 oz Orange juice
1 tsp Lemon juice

Directions:

Shake all ingredients with ice. Strain into a cocktail glass and serve.

MARDI GRAS SUN GOD

The colorful Mardi Gras float parade snaked its way along the crowded streets of the city amidst the cheering and laughing people. Everyone was in a happy mood whether they were on one of the floats, marching alongside them in the street, or merely watching the passing parade from buildings.

Mike, Gary and Chad had gone on holiday specifically to attend the Mardi Gras, and they had joined in the fun with the rest of the locals. Although they were not as lavishly dressed as most of the other participants, they did, however, make themselves look good. Mike had decided to wear only a black faux leather swimming costume, black boots and nothing else, except a broad smile and a chiseled body. Mike had spent many years honing his body, and with the help of a little sun-tan oil being rubbed over his well-defined body, he looked stunning.

Gary had decided to go a-la-leather in his chaps, leather pouch, harness, black cap and boots, while Chad contrasted this in a little red sequined waistcoat and matching red G-string. Fortunately for them, the evening was warm, so at least they didn't develop goose-bumps. The three friends had decided to march together in the parade, but had made a pact that at the after-party, if any of them found someone for the night, they would all go their own ways and meet again the next morning for breakfast.

When the three had first arrived in the city at the start of their holiday, they had booked into their hotel and then made a tour of the city, finding the bars, clubs and beaches. Once these had been established, they spent most of their days on the beach and their evenings in the bars and clubs.

It was while they were at the beach one day that Mike had spotted a very hunky-looking lifeguard. Mike had always been attracted to other guys with a similar physical build to his own, and had started talking to him. The lifeguard's name was Grant and he seemed friendly, but not over friendly. Mike had introduced him to Chad and Gary, and every time they went to the beach and saw Grant, they spoke to him, but that was as far as it went. Chad and Gary could see that Mike was interested in Grant and so didn't make a play for the guy, but they both admired his good looks and physical sexuality that exuded from him.

One evening the three had arranged to meet Grant for a drink at their hotel. He arrived in a well-cut pair of jeans and a white T-shirt. His well-tanned face and arms were off-set by the whiteness of his shirt, and all three admitted that he really was worth chasing after. The more the evening dragged on, the more they plied drinks to Grant, but if it was their intention to try to get him drunk, they were not succeeding. Eventually, after spending a pleasant evening with the three guys, Grant said goodnight to them and made his way home, alone!

As the day of the parade neared, the three had been busy planning what they were going to wear and do on the night, so less time was spent on the beach. However, they did manage to see Grant occasionally, because it was he who told them where they could get some of the items needed for their outfits for the parade.

The afternoon of the parade, Mike had gone to a local gym to pump some iron and build up his body for the evening. When he returned to the hotel, they dressed and Mike got Chad to help rub some of the oil on his back and legs and then the three friends set off for the start of the parade.

While they were marching through the streets, a float decorated to represent an Inca temple overtook them, and standing at the top of the towering temple was a Sun God. He was dressed only in a gold G-String, gold boots, a gold chain around his neck and a very ornate golden mask depicting the sun with its rays emanating from the face. Gary was the first to spot the float with the Sun God.

"Wow, check that float! It's great!"

"Never mind the float," replied Chad, "take a look at the Sun God. I wouldn't mind being sacrificed to him."

Mike spotted what they were looking at, and immediately his attention was grasped. He sped up to the float and looked up at the God, walking at the same pace that the float was traveling. He smiled up at the God, but he was unable to know whether his smile was being returned because the God's face was hidden by the mask. Chad and Gary ran to keep up with Mike, who was now in another world. He couldn't take his eyes off this beautiful body as it rode majestically aloft the temple.

The three marched alongside the Inca Temple float for the rest of the parade until they reached the end of the parade. At the end of the parade, which happened to be where the after-party was also being held, the Sun God dismounted from the float, but before Mike had a chance to go up to him and speak, the man disappeared into the crowd.

"Damn it!" exclaimed Mike, when he lost sight of the man. "Where did he go?"

Neither Chad nor Gary had seen in which direction the young man had gone, so they were of no use to Mike.

The three made their way into one of the marquee tents, which housed a band and bar. They ordered some drinks and settled down to enjoy the music and dance the night away.

A young guy dressed in a sequined pair of pants came up to Chad and said, "Do you want to tangle with my spangles?"

Chad looked at the others, who were about to burst into laughter at this opening line, looked back at the young man, and replied that he would, so off he disappeared onto he dance floor. Soon afterwards, another young guy in leather, with a dog collar around his neck walked up to Gary and asked if he needed a slave. Although Gary was not into S & M, he looked at the young man and decided that he was worth having as a slave, so he took hold of his dog collar and chain and led him off onto the dance floor. Mike stood alone watching everybody enjoying themselves. While he stood there, he became aware of a feeling of being watched. He turned around slowly, surveying the crowd in the tent, until his eyes focused on the shining mask of the Sun God at the far end of the tent. The man stood on a platform, raised sufficiently high enough for him to survey the entire surroundings. Mike immediately started heading in the man's direction. When he arrived at the platform, he stood gazing up at the beautiful torso of this God-like creature. Mike could see from below, that the bulge in the young man's G-String was mammoth, and he stood with his hands on his hips, almost thrusting his pelvis forward as Mike looked up at him. Mike, being closer to him than he was when they were in the parade, could see the eyes of the man looking at him through the mask.

"Would you like a drink," shouted Mike above the sound of the music.

The man nodded, but didn't move.

"Should we go to one of the quieter tents?" asked Mike.

The man nodded again, but this time, he started to climb down from the platform.

Mike led the way out of the tent and headed towards another, where there was less noise.

When they entered the new tent, although there were just as many people as in the last tent, the atmosphere was less hectic and one could hear oneself talk. Mike led the young man over to the bar and asked what he would like to drink.

"A cold drink," came the muffled voice through the mouthpiece of the mask, "with a straw."

The drinks arrived and the young man placed the straw through the mouth opening of his mask and drank. Mike watched and noticed that the man had the most incredibly blue eyes peering through the eye slits in the mask.

"You've got a beautiful body," said Mike.

"Thank you, and so have you. You've obviously trained for some time."

"Yeah for quite a few years," replied Mike.

"I noticed that you marched with our float throughout the parade, why?"

"I'm afraid that this is embarrassing, but when I saw you, I just had to stay near you," said Mike, blushing as he said so.

"I take that as a compliment, but unfortunately, you couldn't see my reactions to you through this mask."

"So why don't you take it off?" asked Mike.

"I think I'd prefer to keep it on until the evening is over," he replied.

"I'd like to invite you back to my place," said Mike, "but I'm sharing with two other guys."

"Are they your lovers?"

"No!" laughed Mike. "They're just very good friends who I can rely on."

"Why don't you come back to my place, then?" asked the young man.

"That would be great. If I could."

So it was decided that Mike was going to spend the evening with his Sun God.

They made their way back to the young man's apartment, still dressed as they had been.

When they arrived inside the apartment, Mike was surprised to see how homely the apartment appeared, but he couldn't see any indications as to who the young man was. They went into the lounge and the young man threw himself into the couch and stretched out his legs. Mike stood admiring the young man's beauty. Although his body was not as defined as Mike's, there was a beauty that Mike couldn't explain.

Mike knelt in front of the young man and ran a hand up his smooth, muscular leg until it reached the edge of the young man's gold G-String. Mike's fingers gently touched the lower part of the G-String where the young man's balls were lying. He ran a finger over them and could feel their solidness. Mike looked up and could see the clear blue eyes watching him. Mike let his fingers travel gently up and over the huge bulge that was covered in gold satin material. Mike heard a slight gasp emit from behind the mask and he saw the blue eyes close as if in pleasure. He continued to run his fingers over the bulge, noticing it growing in size.

"Do you like that?" whispered Mike.

"Mmm!" groaned the young man. "Take it," he said.

Mike slowly pulled down the top of the G-String, allowing the young man's huge dick freedom to escape the confines of the satin. Mike admired the man's throbbing dick and lowered his mouth. His tongue shot out and licked the length of the man's dick until he had wet its entire length, then he swallowed it to the base in one movement. The man gasped aloud and thrust his hips upwards.

"Oh, that's good," he groaned.

Mike continued to work the length of the man's dick, allowing himself as much pleasure as he gave the young man.

The young man suddenly pushed Mike's head from his dick and stood up. He beckoned Mike to follow and led him towards the bedroom.

In the bedroom was a double bed, onto which Mike was pushed. The young man switched off the bedroom light and removed his mask, but Mike couldn't see the face in the dark. Mike lay on his back while the young man pulled Mike's faux leather costume down to his ankles, allowing Mike to kick them off, then he went down on Mike's cock, lathering it with his saliva. He worked his way around Mike's balls, taking each one into his mouth and gently rolling it around his mouth before allowing it to escape and taking in the other one. He then lifted Mike's legs into the air and headed his tongue in the direction of Mike's ass. Mike's cock began to throb in anticipation of what was to come. Mike groaned ecstatically when the young man's tongue hit his asshole.

While he attacked Mike's asshole, the young man pulled his G-String off and started playing with his own dick. Eventually, he removed his head from Mike, pulled Mike's legs onto his own muscular shoulders and aimed his huge cock at the entrance to Mike's asshole. Mike's six-pack abdomen tensed as the young man's cock slowly touched Mike's pucker. The young man pushed gently forward and Mike gave in, allowing full entry. Mike groaned with pleasure, as the young man penetrated him.

The young man sighed with absolute contentment as he entered Mike and held his position for a while. Once Mike had become used to the huge size of the young man, he started to ride the young man's cock, encouraging him to penetrate deeper with each thrust.

Mike's muscular thighs wrapped around the young man, pulling the man's cock deeper into his ass. Mike took hold of the young man's nipples and squeezed them, causing the young man to thrust even deeper and harder. This obviously turned the young man on, thought Mike, so he continued to do this, twisting and pinching the young man's nipples. Mike could feel that the young man's pace was increasing. His thrusts were becoming more frantic and Mike knew that his new friend was getting ready to explode and empty his love juice into the depths of his ass. Mike was enjoying this feeling and he wanted his young man to feel the same, so he tightened his ass muscles, clamping tightly around the young man's cock. The young man gave a cry and Mike could feel the warm vibrations erupting inside of him. The young man pounded with fury as he emptied his load. As the last drops of his hot cum were sent into the depths of Mike, he slumped onto Mike's stomach and took Mike's cock into his mouth.

This kid had stamina, thought Mike, as the young man frantically worked up and down the length of Mike's cock. Mike could feel himself getting closer to the edge.

"I'm gonna come," shouted Mike.

"Shoot," gasped the young man, speeding up his action.

Mike fired shot after shot, which the young man swallowed as furiously as it was shot into his mouth. When Mike had finished shooting, the young man still did not let go of Mike's cock, but milked it dry, sucking and kissing it. Then he released Mike's cock from his mouth and slowly slid up the length of Mike's body until his mouth reached Mike's and they started to kiss. Mike could taste the saltiness of his own cum in the young man's mouth and this turned him on. He could feel his cock beginning to react again, but he desperately wanted to know who his Sun God was, so that he could at least have a name to use.

"Please tell me who you are?" asked Mike.

"Are you sure that you want to know?" came the reply. "If so, put on the light."

Mike leapt from the bed and went to the light switch. As he switched on the light, he looked over to the bed and there lay Grant.

"Grant! I don't believe this. I thought you were straight, being a lifeguard!"

Mike's face was a picture of surprise at seeing Grant lying on the bed.

"Of all the people who I would want to take to bed, you have always been my choice ever since I first saw you, and now I've done it."

"Well, it doesn't end there," said Grant, "ever since I saw you I wanted you, so if you're game and you want it, my ass is waiting for you."

"You mean…?"

"Yeah, I've wanted that body of yours ramming my tight ass and filling me with your juice. Do you want it?"

"You bet," was Mike's reply and he proceeded to kiss Grant all over, sucking on his nipples and getting Grant's cock hard again.

The following morning, they awoke in each other's arms, having spent the night making love to each other. When Mike went off to meet Chad and Gary for breakfast, he took Grant with him.

"Hi, Mike," said Gary, "did you meet Grant on the way here?"

Grant and Mike smiled to each other.

"No, actually I met him last night, so I invited him for breakfast with us this morning."

Nothing more was said, but when they ordered their breakfast, the waiter asked Mike how he would like his egg, "Sun God side up," replied Mike, smiling at Grant.

Immediately Chad and Gary grasped what had happened the previous night.

"You mean this is your Sun God?" asked Chad.

"Yeah," replied Mike, "our very own lifeguard!

- **RAIDER** -

Ingredients:

½ oz Bailey's Irish Cream
½ oz Cointreau
½ oz Grand Marnier

Directions:

Layer the ingredients in order in a shot glass.

BREAK-IN

Gary and Gloria Stansky had grown up together, been to the same school and had eventually married, much to both sets of parents delight. They had been married for three years and could be considered a very average married couple, both continuing to work and delaying starting a family because their careers were important to each of them. Their day-to-day lives tended to be very ordinary and their circle of friends was small, so they didn't often go out at night, except to see the odd film.

One evening, Gary and Gloria were asleep in bed when Gloria awoke to hear a sound downstairs. She gently shook Gary to waken him.

"Gary! Gary, I think there's someone downstairs."

Gary gave a grunt and turned over in bed. Again Gloria shook him and whispered in his ear that she thought someone was downstairs. Eventually Gary woke up and both he and Gloria got out of bed. Slowly they made their way downstairs in the dark. Gloria had put on a dressing gown, but Gary remained in his sleeping shorts and carried only a baseball bat as defense. They slowly descended the stairs and quietly entered the lounge. Immediately on entering the lounge, Gary switched on the lounge light, confronting their burglar who was dressed from head to foot in black and had his face covered with a ski-mask.

"Stand where you are and put up your hands," shouted Gary, waving the baseball bat. The burglar froze where he was standing, not a muscle moved.

"Gloria, go and phone the police."

"I'm not leaving you in case there's another burglar in the house."

"In that case you stay here and guard him, while I go and call the police."

Gary handed over the baseball bat and left the lounge to go to the phone which was in the hallway.

While he was out, Gloria moved in front of the burglar, staring at the eyes peering through the ski-mask.

"Who are you and what do you want?" she asked.

There was no response.

Slowly she edged a little closer to the burglar and tried to peer through the ski-mask, but could obviously only see the burglar's eyes and mouth. She stared into a pair of steely-blue eyes staring back at her. She stretched forward and took hold of the ski-mask which she ripped from his head. The minute that the mask had revealed the burglar's face than he grabbed Gloria, put a hand over her mouth to prevent her from screaming and disarmed her of the baseball bat. He then frog-marched her towards the lounge curtains where he took two of the tie-back cords which were attached to the curtains, and with one hand, tied Gloria's arms behind her back. He then found a roll of packing tape lying on a sideboard in the lounge, tore off a strip and placed that over her mouth. He then gently maneuvered her towards a wingback chair, seated her down and tied her to the chair by means of the remaining tie-back cords.

"Gloria, I can't get through to the police, the line must be cut," said Gary re-entering the lounge, only to find Gloria bound and gagged in the wingback chair. The burglar stood, armed with the baseball bat, in the centre of the lounge.

"Sit!" hissed the burglar to Gary.

"What the hell's going on here?" shouted Gary advancing towards the burglar.

The burglar merely prodded Gary in the stomach with the baseball bat, temporarily winding him.

"I said sit!" hissed the burglar again.

By now Gary was sitting on the couch, which had its back to the wingback in which Gloria was seated. The burglar stared down at Gary and Gary reciprocated the look.

The burglar must have been close to six-foot three tall with a muscular body and a rugged, weather-beaten face, full lips and steely-blue eyes. Gary surveyed the man's stature and realized that although he was fairly well-built, he would probably be no match for the burglar.

"Please take what you want and go," said Gary, from the couch.

From Gloria came a muffled sound as though to echo Gary's request.

The burglar placed the baseball bat on the coffee table and stood in front of Gary, hands tucked into the waist of his black jeans with his hands splayed across his crotch. This became a focal point and Gary's eyes were attracted to this area. He could see that under the cloth of the jeans lay a bulge of enormous magnitude. The burglar slowly rubbed his hands across his bulging crotch and as he did so, Gary could feel his own cock becoming aroused in his sleeping shorts. The burglar stood and watched as Gary's cock slowly began to grow and thicken, rising to produce what looked like a tent-pole supporting the soft material of his shorts.

The burglar advanced towards Gary and, taking hold of the waistband of Gary's sleeping shorts with his huge hands, pulled them down over Gary's knees, freeing his throbbing cock. Gary sat on the couch revealing himself to the burglar, but where Gloria could not see. She knew what the burglar had done, and she tried to say something as he had done so. She was trying desperately to free herself, but was unable to do so.

The burglar moved to between Gary's legs and knelt. He held Gary's cock in his hand and squeezed its swollen stem while his other hand fondled Gary's balls. As he did so, Gary groaned, pleasurably. The burglar licked the tip of the mushroomed head and circled its rim with his tongue, then proceeded to run his tongue down the length of Gary's cock until he reached his balls, all the while staring into Gary's eyes. He licked on one, rolling it into his mouth and sucking gently on it, and then he repeated the same action on the other one. Throughout this whole motion, Gary lay back transfixed, groaning in pleasure while Gloria continued to give muffled sounds from the wingback chair. From where she was sitting she could only imagine what was happening to Gary.

Gary enjoyed the pleasure he was receiving for a while, then he leant forward and removed the burglar's black top to reveal a well-developed chest with two swollen nipples mounted on a pair of firm pectoral muscles and a stomach rippling with muscles. Gary gasped at the sight and his cock bobbed with excitement. The burglar went back to sucking on Gary's cock while Gary proceeded to pinch the burglar's nipples, sending shockwaves through the burglar's body.

After some time, the burglar rose from between Gary's legs and undid his jeans. As he slid them to the floor, Gloria's eyes widened as she saw the bulge packed into a white jock-strap and the muscular legs. The burglar stepped from his jeans and stood in front of Gary, thrusting his crotch in Gary's face, allowing his mouth to kiss the heavy package that the burglar carried. Gary rubbed his nose along the solid length in the jock-strap and smelt the musky-sweet smell of sweat, man and piss. Using his teeth, Gary pulled the jock-strap lower to release the shining head of the burglar's engorged cock from its constraints. The burglar's cock rose to the occasion and Gary could not resist the opportunity and took the burglar's cock into his mouth and swallowed it down to the base where his chin rubbed up against the soft fur on the burglar's balls. He held his position, luxuriating in the taste of the man's cock, then slowly began to withdraw his mouth. The burglar gave a slight sneer as Gary did this and then thrust his cock down Gary's throat, almost gagging him.

The burglar watched Gary's face intently and could see the pleasure and enjoyment that Gary was experiencing from his actions. By this time, Gloria was well aware of what was happening, but because she could not see Gary's face, was unaware of the pleasure that the burglar's cock was giving him. Gary fondled the burglar's balls, gently rolling them in the palms of his hands and ever so gently squeezing them every now and then.

After what seemed an eternity to Gary, the burglar pulled out of Gary's mouth, bent down to his jeans and pulled out a condom which he removed from its foil container and unrolled it onto his full length. He then pulled Gary to the edge of the couch and began licking the area between Gary's balls and his asshole. Gary groaned loudly as the burglar's tongue ventured closer to that magic hole. On finding it, the burglar pushed his tongue into its waiting entrance and felt Gary's muscles clamp on his tongue. He flicked his tongue, teasingly, lubricating Gary's pucker all the while. When he felt that he had lubricated it enough, he stood up, pulled Gary's legs up into the air and guided his long cock towards its destination.

As the burglar pushed into Gary, Gloria tried desperately to get out of her chair to protect her husband, but Gary didn't want protection, he desperately wanted that enormous cock to be buried inside of him and to feel it throbbing there. Although the burglar was muscular and rugged-looking, his actions to Gary at this moment were tender and gentle. He slid his cock slowly into the warmth that Gary generated until it could go no further and he felt his balls rub up against Gary's ass. He then proceeded to develop a rhythm which pleased both him and Gary.

Gary lay on the couch, eyes closed in euphoria and groaned softly as the burglar plunged into and withdrew from Gary's pulsating asshole. At one stage, the burglar withdrew his cock until only the mushroom head was hidden, and using short thrusts, massaged his cock-head against Gary's prostate. Gary's cock was leaking pre-cum and he was writhing in ecstasy the more the burglar continued his action. The burglar knew that he was bringing Gary to the very edge and he could feel his own balls riding up into his ball sac, ready to shoot his load.

"I'm going to come," groaned Gary, looking lovingly into the steel-blue eyes of his aggressor.

The burglar gave a sudden deep thrust, tensed and both men began to fire their loads. The burglar could feel the contractions as Gary's cock throbbed and fired load after load of warm cum onto his chest and stomach. The burglar held firmly onto Gary's legs, pulling him deeper onto his cock and thrusting violently, grunting loudly with each thrust. Both men's bodies glistened with perspiration in the lounge light.

What went through Gloria's mind as the two men came, we will never know, but she never lost the frightened rabbit stare throughout the burglar and Gary's sexual intercourse. After both men had exhausted themselves, the burglar leant across Gary's stomach, placed his lips on Gary's and sucked on Gary's tongue, pulling it into his mouth and feeling Gary's cock throbbing again as he did so. Their lips parted and slowly the large bargepole was pulled from its warm protection in Gary. As the burglar's cock slipped free, Gary gave a sigh, smiled and his whole body relaxed.

The burglar smiled at Gary, took the condom off, filled with his love juice and left it on the couch next to Gary, pulled on his jock-strap, stuffing his still engorged cock into its stretch material, put on his shirt and jeans, blew a kiss to Gloria, walked out of the lounge, switched off the lights and disappeared.

Gloria became desperate to free herself and was making an overwhelming amount of noise through the tape covering her mouth. Gary lay on the couch with a satisfied smile on his face as if in a trance. Eventually, Gloria's grunting and moaning brought him back to reality and he leapt up from the couch, switched the lounge lights back on and began to free Gloria. His cock was still half hard and he still had the evidence of his cum on his chest and stomach. He ripped off the tape covering Gloria's mouth and the muttered sounds became verbalized.

"What the fuck were you doing?" she screamed at him.

"If I didn't do as he said, he could have killed us," was Gary's reply.

"…and what about me?"

"What about you? Just think what I've been through," said Gary sounding sorry for himself.

"By the sounds of it I think you were enjoying yourself."

"Of course I wasn't. Do you know how painful it was with that huge cock of his?"

"Well, I'm not going to argue with you, call the police."

"You know I can't; I told you that the line was down, probably cut," came Gary's reply.

"Well we've got to notify them somehow!"

"I'll take a drive to the police station and report it," said Gary, "but you stay here, you've had enough for one night."

Gary pulled on his sleeping shorts over his continually diminishing cock and headed out to the car, leaving Gloria in the safety of the house. He got into the driver's seat, stretched across to the glove compartment and took out some tissues to wipe away the evidence from his chest and stomach, switched on the headlamps and in the light he saw a piece of paper on the windscreen. He got out of the car, took the paper and read:

> ***Thanks, that was great. If you ever want to***
> ***do it again phone 325784.***

Gary's cock gave a little twitch; he smiled, folded the paper and placed it in the glove compartment of his car.

- DARK SANGAREE -

Ingredients:

¾ cup dark beer (chilled)
3 tbsp club soda or mineral water
1 tsp sugar syrup
Freshly grated nutmeg

Directions:

Pour the beer into a highball glass. Top with soda or mineral water. Sweeten with syrup and spice with nutmeg. Stir.

IN THE DARK

Going into Mick's bookstore was always interesting, not only for its selection of books, but also for what went on behind its famous, yet to some, infamous, black door. When one passed through the front door, which was painted a bright yellow, suggesting sunshine and warmth, the first attack on the senses was the mustiness which pervaded the store. It wasn't a particularly unpleasant odor, but one which was particularly associated with old books, and one which soon grew on a person, literally. Apart from the brightly painted front door, almost hidden behind the many shelves of books, was a door painted black at the far end of the store on which was painted the word 'Private' in white. The very word 'private' conjured up ideas of mystery. To most people, they assumed that this area was reserved for the staff, as would be found in most shops. However, those in the know would greet Mick; perhaps have a lingering look at some of the books on the shelves, then venture through the 'private' black door, to emerge some time later.

I wandered into the store on this particular Saturday evening and saw Mick behind the counter, serving a customer. I made my way to one of the shelves and searched the titles of some of the new arrivals, while Mick busied himself with the customer. Once the customer had paid for his books and departed, I stopped to chat to Mick.

A couple of other customers were busy browsing along the shelves in search of their desired fiction or non-fiction, whichever took their fancy.

"How's business today?" I enquired, knowing that Mick knew to what I was referring.

"Busy, Pete," came the sprightly reply and Mick smiled a knowing smile.

I knew precisely to what he was referring, so I first glanced at the other customers, and then strode towards the black door at the rear of the shop.

As I opened the black door, the light from the store flooded the darkened area behind the door. I walked through and closed the door behind me. Blackness enveloped me as I stood trying to let my eyes adjust to the darkness; not that it would make any difference as the only light that filtered through came from the small crack under the bottom of the door. As I breathed in the air behind the black door, I noticed it took on a different aroma, if one could call it that. The musty smell of books seemed to have been swathed in a smell found only on humans; the odor of sweat mixed inextricably with deodorant.

I stood there for a minute taking in the encompassing odors, and then felt for the wall. Its coldness welcomed my fingertips. Slowly I inched my way along the wall in the dark, breathing gently and taking in the fumes of deodorant which came stronger as I moved along. I could hear faint movements but couldn't establish exactly where the sounds were coming from.

My hand edged along the wall until it came to a halt as I felt someone standing against the wall. My hand felt the shoulder and then instinctively ran down to the bicep. It was muscular, which I liked, so I stood my ground. I felt two reciprocating hands touch me. The hands seemed firm to the touch and then slid down my sides to my waist. After a moment, they then traveled back up to my shoulders, neck and face.

"You haven't been here long," whispered a voice close to my ear.

"I beg your pardon?" I whispered back to the mysterious voice from the gloom.

"I can smell that you haven't," came the deep yet, soft voice.

"I'm sorry, I don't understand," I responded, equally quietly.

"You smell fresh. You haven't acquired the store's mustiness or the smells that permeate in this back area."

I breathed in deeply and smelt a strong, lingering scent of aftershave. I wanted to go up closer to where I smelt the aroma, possibly to try to identify the brand, but I refrained from doing so.

My contact's hands traced the shape of my face, and then moved to my hair.

"You're good-looking," said the voice.

I stood frozen in time, wondering to myself, *how could he see whether I was good-looking, here in the dark?*

I raised my hands to where I thought the mysterious man was standing. My hands ran over two well-formed pectoral muscles with two protruding nipples within the confines of a tightly fitting silk shirt. I leant closer to him and caught the musty odor of the books, which mingled subtly with his aftershave, so I assumed he'd been here for some time.

We stood together in the darkness, my hands on his pecs and his hands on my face. As we stood there, other bodies bumped into us but moved on without a word being spoken. There seemed to be a passive silence, the sort of thing one might find in a library or even a church. Nobody spoke. The movement of people's feet was the only thing that could be heard, and then it was of a quiet nature.

I felt a hand leave my face and head to my crotch. It caressed my jeans, warming my ever-burgeoning cock. The hand traced the outline of my cock through my jeans and then gave my crotch a gentle, but firm squeeze. The thought of the unknown man turned me on.

"You're cut, and that's how I like a cock," said the voice in my ear.

I froze where I stood. How could he tell through the material of my jeans? I felt his warm breath close to my neck, and smelt the invigorating aroma of his aftershave, then the roughness of his tongue tip being inserted into my ear. I felt it travel in and around my ear and then to my neck. Goose bumps developed along the length of my arms as his tongue made its way around my ears, first the left and then the right.

The silence was soon broken by the sound of the zip of my jeans slowly being lowered, and then his firm hands entered the opening of my jeans and began to free my hardened cock from the confines of my jeans and briefs. His tongue had left my ears and I felt the warmth of his mouth as he engulfed my cock-head and began salivating up and down the length of my stem. The feeling of his warmth caused me to sigh deeply and I instinctively gave a gentle thrust with my hips. Somehow I felt safe in the dark with him.

He then stopped.

Again a voice came to my ear.

"Come with me, someone's coming," he said, taking my hand and leading me through the darkness. I never heard anyone coming near us, but I soon bumped into some bodies and hands felt my body in search of my cock, which was still protruding from my jeans. A hand grasped my erection and jerked it a couple of times but before anything untoward could take place, my companion's hand pulled me along. I had no idea where we were, other than there were people around me, but I remained clasped to his hand.

Suddenly we came to a halt.

I stood motionless and silent, my guide having released his grasp on my hand.

Once again, I felt the warm mouth coating my cock with licks and kisses. I knew it was him by the gentle caressing of his mouth. I rested my hands on my companion's shoulders, and then moved them up to his head. I could feel that he had short-cropped hair. I ran my finger through his hair and then pulled his head onto my cock until I felt his lips around the base of my cock. It felt good to be deep down his throat. I held this position for a while, luxuriating in his warmth and the movement of his tongue as he rubbed the underside of my cock stem with it.

The suction that he created with his mouth made me feel as though he was ready to swallow my whole being.

After a while, he slowly slid his mouth along my solid muscle until I felt the tip of my cock almost slip from his mouth. I thrust forward, not wanting to lose contact with him. Once more he slid his mouth down my length, letting the roughness of his tongue tease the underside of my cock, thereby creating a tingling affect throughout my body. I held onto his cropped head, pulling it onto my cock and then releasing him to slide back to the tip. All the while I could hear movement of people.

I felt his fingers grasp my ass and squeeze my ass cheeks, and at the same time, start pulling my jeans and my briefs down to my ankles. Once my butt was bare, his warm hands began massaging both cheeks, pulling me closer into his throat. His deft fingers worked their way around my ass in search of my entrance. His finger tips caressed my crack, tickling my entrance and causing me to automatically clamp my asshole shut. His fingers massaged over my hole, allowing me to relax and allowing him entry. A finger gently penetrated the barrier to my being, causing me to gasp, but I had not intention of forbidding him entrance; in fact I welcomed him in like a guest. His finger sank deeper into me and then began a gentle rotation as it searched my inner being. All the while I sighed and gasped with each movement that he made. I also knew that others were gathering near to us because other hands began searching my body, but I didn't want them.

My companion's hand slowly began to retreat from its hidden cavity. I clamped my muscle in a desperate attempt to prevent him from leaving, but no sooner had he freed himself from me, than I felt two fingers enter and search me. As both spread my ass wider and rotated in me, I felt my balls rising and I thought I might erupt with pleasure, but I didn't want this to end so soon.

I put my arms under his armpits and lifted him from his kneeling position. I let my hand cup his balls and cock which were still well hidden in his jeans. I unzipped his jeans and began to reciprocate with my mouth. It felt good to have his long uncut cock deep in my throat as I felt the gentle thrusts. I wanted to please him as much as he'd pleased me.

My mouth worked long and hard along his thick stem as I washed it with my tongue. His pendulous, manly balls hung below his thick cock, waiting to be warmed and lubricated. I massaged them with my hands and at the same time licked and sucked on each in turn, feeling their wondrous size being engulfed in my mouth.

His breathing became more intense and quickened. I knew that he was close to shooting his load. It didn't take him long to reach his climax. I felt the gentle, light touches of his hands on my face and head as he fired his load. The stream flowed and I swallowed. I felt each thrust and throb as he fired load after load down my throat. When I had extracted every last drop from him, the large, but gentle hands lifted me to my feet.

"Thanks," he breathed into my ear. "That was fantastic, but now it's your turn."

His hands slid down my torso as he made his way back to my cock. The warm suction was clamped tightly around the full length of my cock and I felt his tongue lubricating my stem once more.

His coming and shooting into my mouth had brought me closer to my own orgasm and as his mouth tightened around my cock, I gave a grunt, tensed and fired. I don't think he tasted any of my cum because my cock-head was right at the back of his throat, so my fill must have gone straight down his throat. My groans were loud, attracting others to come closer to us.

His tongue licked and cleaned me of all evidence and it was only once my cock had begun to subside, that I was able to withdraw from his warmth and lift him to his feet again.

Once we'd finished, we both zipped up and I said, "How do we get out of here in the dark?"

"Take my hand and I'll lead you."

Although I'd been in the dark backroom for quite some time, I still hadn't got used to the dark and I still couldn't see anything in front of me, but could feel his presence. Again we passed people and again hands stretched out to grope.

Suddenly the black door opened and the brightness of the lights in the store blinded me momentarily. I looked at my companion. He must have been at least six feet tall, well-built and good-looking. As we entered the light of the bookstore, I turned to him and introduced myself.

"By the way, my name's Pete," I said, stretching out my hand to shake his.

"Hi Pete, I'm Kurt," he replied, but didn't take my hand. Then reality hit me. Kurt couldn't see me, he was blind.

- ICEBERG -

Ingredients:

1 oz White Crème de Menthe
½ oz Peppermint Schnapps
½ oz Goldschlager
Fill with milk

Directions:

Pour ingredients over ice in a blender. Blend and then pour into a chilled highball glass. Garnish with chocolate shavings.

DESSERT UNDER WRAPS

Monday night was not a busy night at *Ravioli's*, my favorite restaurant. In fact, by 9.30 p.m Mike and I were the only customers in the restaurant.

Mike had asked me to meet him as he and his boyfriend, Chad, had a fight that day and things were not currently going well in their relationship. I agreed to meet with him and suggested we go to *Ravioli's*.

As we were the only people there, we'd decided to spend a long evening together and had gone through the starters and the main course, Mike filling me in as to what was going wrong with their relationship while we ploughed through the menu. It was obviously clear to me that although Mike loved Chad, he felt that Chad was smothering him.

"I can't go out with my friends and I have to tell him everywhere I go," bemoaned Mike.

"Well, perhaps he worries about you and he's thinking only of your safety," I suggested.

"It's just that I want some space sometimes," he continued.

"Have you ever told him about your need for space?" I asked, thinking that this would have been the obvious thing to do.

"No," was the reply, much to my surprise.

We discussed aspects of their relationship so I could establish if it was a one-sided problem or that in fact, they were both guilty of this breakdown.

The waiter arrived and we ordered dessert: Crème Brûlée for Mike and my favorite, ice cream and chocolate sauce. As the waiter departed, we continued our conversation for a while, when I suddenly looked up and saw Chad about to enter the restaurant.

"Mike, Chad's here," I gasped. "He's coming into the restaurant."

"Oh shit, he'll think I'm two-timing him."

At this, Mike did what he thought was the most obvious thing to do; he slid from his chair and darted under the table at which we were sitting and quietly sat still on the floor. Fortunately the tables at *Ravioli's* always prided themselves in having long table cloths which covered their table tops and reached the floor.

"Don't say a word that I'm here," hissed Mike from under the table.

Chad looked around the restaurant and, as there were no other patrons, I stood out like a proverbial sore thumb.

"Hi Pete," he said, crossing towards the table. "Have you seen Mike at all?"

What do I say now? Do I say 'yes, he's hiding under the table'? I felt Mike tap my leg.

"Hi Chad, he was here earlier, but he's left."

What I do for friends!

"Do you mind if I sit?"

"Not at all," I replied, not knowing how much scuttling Mike was having to do under the table.

Chad sat and began to tell me his side of the story; how much he loved Mike but admitted to being extremely jealous because of Mike's good looks. He felt that with these good looks, he was going to lose Mike to someone else.

"I'm sure he's whoring around town as we sit here," said Chad thumping the table with his fist, making the salt and pepper sets reverberate on the table top.

"Oh I'm sure he's not," I replied, trying to defuse Chad's anger. Just then I felt a hand, obviously Mike's, slowly slide up my left leg until it reached my crotch where his nimble fingers began to unzip the zipper to my jeans. I must have had a bit of a surprised look on my face because Chad asked if anything was wrong, but I assured him that everything was just fine.

I felt my limp cock being extracted from the confines of my briefs and a warm mouth surrounding it. My eyes widened as I froze in my sitting position and felt the activities between my legs.

"What's the problem?" enquired Chad, seeing my expression.

"No problem," I stammered, "it's just a twinge I felt in my stomach."

"Pete, do you think Mike's off with some other guy?"

"I'm sure he's not off with someone, in fact he's probably on his way home," I said, rather loudly, hoping that Mike would hear and get the message.

"I really don't think he's aware of how much I feel for him," continued Chad, as I tried to maintain my decorum.

Just then the waiter arrived with desserts. He placed the ice cream in front of me and as he placed the Crème Brûlée in front of Chad, their eyes met. The surprise in the waiter's face to see a different person sitting there was probably no different from the surprise expressed on my face as Mike's mouth sank down my hardened cock, engulfing my entire length. The waiter hovered at the table then returned to the kitchen leaving Chad bewildered at having a dessert placed in front of him.

"I didn't order this," said Chad, still looking puzzled.

I had to think quickly.

"No, Mike ordered it before he left, but they were so long in bringing it, so why don't you eat it?"

I dipped my spoon into my ice cream, inserted it into my mouth just as Mike clamped his mouth tightly around my cock and sucked. I gasped loudly. Chad stared at me.

"The ice cream – it's cold," I said, trying to use that as the excuse for my gasping.

Chad started tucking into the Crème Brûlée as Mike started to tuck into his dessert under the table. This was not the first time that Mike and I had enjoyed a scene together, but not in public, and I knew how skilled he was in the use of that mouth of his; so skilled in fact that, given the opportunity, he could get a guy off within a minute. I was desperately trying to think of other things rather than what was happening beneath the wraps of the table. Chad, in between enjoying his dessert, continued to extol the merits and demerits of Mike.

At one stage, a loud sucking sound emanated from beneath the table, so I quickly placed my spoon on my mouth and imitated the sound, in the hopes that Chad would think it originated from me.

I could feel myself getting closer and closer and Mike knew it because he increased his pace. I started to become fidgety, trying to adjust my position in my seat, but without making it too obvious to Chad that something was not quite kosher.

Chad finished his dessert, placed his spoon in his dish and pushed it aside. The moment of truth was nearing and I was sure that the expression on my face was giving me away. I lifted my spoon with ice cream to my mouth and as its coolness entered my mouth, so my warmth entered Mike's mouth.

Instantly and uncontrollably I groaned in ecstasy as I shot my load down Mike's throat. Chad looked at me and with my eyes closed I pretended that the taste of the ice cream and chocolate sauce was the cause of my ecstasy. I opened my eyes, caught him watching me, smacked my lips together and said, "Hmm! That was so delicious. Eating ice cream and chocolate sauce is just like having sex," and smiled at Chad.

He looked suspiciously at me and asked, "Are you OK?"

"Why?" I replied, still smiling contentedly.

"You look flushed."

"Like I say, eating ice cream is like having sex. It does this to me."

The waiter had returned from the kitchen, hovered, then picked up the empty dishes, looked strangely at my sublime face that smiled at him and then I said, "Could I have the bill please?"

He duly brought it. As I was paying, I felt my now subsiding cock being placed back in my briefs and my jeans being zipped up again.

"Shall we go, Chad," I said, rising from my chair.

"Pete, I think you've spilled a bit of ice cream on your jeans."

I looked down at the white evidence and without missing a beat said, "Oops, you're so right." I scooped it up with a finger and popped the evidence into my mouth allowing the saltiness to mingle with the remnants of ice cream flavors.

As we left *Ravioli's,* to go out into the night, I turned and from the corner of my eye I caught a glimpse of an equally contented young man emerging from under the table.

- BLACK JACK -

Ingredients:

1 oz Yukon Jack
¼ oz Chambord Raspberry liqueur
½ oz Sour mix
Splash of 7-Up

Directions:

Mix all the ingredients together over ice. Shake till very chilled and strain into glasses.

EBONY AND IVORY

Stevie Wonder and Paul McCartney's voices came over my walkman loud and clear as they sang 'Ebony and Ivory' and I lay on my bed in the college dorm, staring up at the ceiling, daydreaming.

The college year had only just begun and lectures were underway. I had been introduced to my new room mate and on that day, I knew my year was going to be just grand. I remember opening our dorm door when I heard the knock and realizing that my jaw was hanging three feet below where it should have been. Joshua Wellington Samuels, or Josh as he was to be known to his friends, stood blocking the doorway. This young white boy gaped at the large black man that blocked the entrance with his broad shoulders and trim waist.

"Hi," I stammered, gawking at this giant of a man, whose shoulders seemed to squeeze through the frame of the doorway.

He looked like a Colossus; thick sturdy legs encased in his track pants, a T-shirt that seemed to be stretched to its limit in an effort to cover his broad chest, and a baseball cap on his head with the peak at the back. His skin was the color of coffee, with milk in it, and his face seemed to radiate warmth. He looked a friendly sort of guy.

"Hi. I'm Josh and I'm your new roomy," he replied, grabbing my hand in a vice-like grip and shaking it. I could feel the pressure being exerted on my hand and wondered if any bones were being crushed. As he squeezed, I could see how his biceps bulged and I also felt the tingle that ran through my body from brain to balls and then up to cock.

Josh was on a sports scholarship and played football, so I knew there were going to be times when I'd probably cream myself looking at him in his jockstrap or football gear, but I was aware that I'd have to be careful and not be too obvious in my desire for this man.

From a small boy, I had always fantasized about the football players I'd seen in the magazines. I would buy the mags only to sit and stare at the guys in their tight outfits and wonder what was under that clothing, and then I'd take hold of my hard-on and stroke myself until I shot a load. Added to my fantasy was the fact that I always thought that the black guys seemed to have bigger packages in their shorts than the white guys, and I imagined myself taking their thick cocks down my throat, and probably gagging in the process.

I had brought a couple of my old football magazines with me to college, for those lonely nights when I had to sort myself out, which I kept in my locker in the room, but chose never to reveal to Josh my interest in the players. Sure, he did ask me if I liked sport and I said that I did, but it wasn't so much the game that interested me as much as the players did.

It must have been about two weeks after the start of the college year that I came home from lectures one afternoon and walked into our dorm. Josh had been to football practice and was lying on his bed, asleep. Now there was nothing out of the ordinary for Josh to have a sleep during the day, except when I saw him on the bed, the word 'Rape!' came into my mind. I wanted to jump the guy there and then, taking his huge cock down my throat first and then ride it until he fired every drop of his seed into my tight little white ass.

Josh was lying on the bed, having removed his top but keeping on his silver-gray tight football shorts. I could distinctly see the massive bulge that lay in the front and the beautifully ripe nipples, waiting to be sucked and chewed. The two mounds of his pectorals rose and fell gently as he breathed and I watched as the tight stomach muscles worked in conjunction with his breathing. I quietly put down my books and went and stood over him, looking down at this beautiful man.

Weakness got the better of me and I knelt down next to the bed. I stretched out a hand and very gently, with my forefinger, touched his right nipple. It felt soft to the touch and I wondered if I could go further and perhaps, give it a tweak. On the other hand, if I did that, he might wake up and hit me, after all, he was very much bigger than me, in all areas. I could feel my cock rising rapidly in my jeans even before I touched his nipple. I ran my finger around his areola and then brushed my finger over his nipple again. This time I could feel a hardening in the nipple. I stood up and leant over Josh so as to take his nipple into my mouth. My tongue licked gently over the tip and then I nibbled it slightly. I released my mouth from his nipple and looked down over his magnificent brown body. There was definitely a change in the size of the package that was encased in the tight silver-gray material.

Josh sighed and adjusted his lying position on the bed slightly. I froze. He turned onto his side so that he was facing me. Once more I knelt next to the bed. But this time temptation was getting the better of me. I looked longingly at the bulging crotch and then decided I couldn't hold back any more.

My tongue slowly licked where his balls would be and then traveled over them and up the length of his shaft, saturating the silky material. I could feel his cock hardening as I covered his length. I continued to slide my tongue up and down his hard cock until I suddenly felt a hand on the back of my head, forcing my mouth onto his cock. At the same time, I felt a gentle thrust of Josh's crotch in my face.

My fingers moved up to his nipples and while my mouth searched along his saturated crotch, so I pinched his hard nipples. A gasp and another thrust greeted me and I became content in the knowledge that my roomy liked what was happening to him.

I stopped salivating on Josh's crotch and looked at him; he was awake and watching me.

"What are you after?" he asked, solemnly.

I had got this far, so I decided it was no use lying to the man because he wouldn't believe me.

"I want that big black cock of yours in this tight white ass of mine," I said, almost in a whisper.

Josh loosened his shorts, allowing me to gain access to his cock. I pulled down his shorts and there was his bulging, white jock strap. It looked so sexy, the white against the coffee color of his smooth skin that I immediately began to salivate over the coarse material with my mouth. His cock had grown both in girth and length and the tip was peeking over the waistband of his jock strap. The cut head was leaking a clear stream of juice, so I stuck out my tongue and licked it up, licking my lips to allow it to spread over my mouth.

"Do you like that?" asked Josh, pulling my head down onto the tip of his black cock.

"Mmm!" I grunted as my mouth clamped tightly over his cock head and pushed the waistband of his jocks down a little to reveal more of his long shaft.

"Take it all," he commanded.

I pulled down his jock strap to release his throbbing cock. I smiled in awe when I saw just how big he was. My own cock gave a couple of throbs and my ass twitched with excitement on seeing his massive size. Now I was even more determined to take this man inside of me.

My mouth worked on his glistening cock, taking it to the back of my throat where it tickled my tonsils, and then sliding my wet lips along its thick shaft until I reached the tip where I received my reward of some clear love juice. Josh began to fuck my face and I found myself not having to exert any effort on his length as he was thrusting back and forth down my throat. I could sense that Josh was enjoying this treatment, but didn't want it to end too soon, so he sat up on the bed and lifted me to my feet.

"Strip, white boy!"

I didn't need an invitation to do that. My shirt, jeans, shoes and socks and briefs disappeared rapidly until I stood white and naked in front of my roomy, my stiff cock looking like a striking cobra in search of something to attack. He removed all the excess clothing he had on and stood in front of me. His cock was far thicker and longer than mine, so it jabbed me in the stomach, coating me with a thin layer of pre-cum. His muscular arms encircled my chest and he squeezed me closer to him until our nipples rubbed together, then he ground his hard cock into my groin. His cock slipped between my legs, so I clamped them tightly together and he began sliding his cock frottage style, while he searched my mouth with his tongue. Our tongues dueled together for some time and then I pulled out of his mouth in order to attack his nipples.

Josh being six-foot-six, meant that I was able to clamp my mouth around each nipple in turn, and work on it, by chewing and nibbling them. Each time I bit into the hard flesh, Josh thrust his cock between my legs and I could feel how his cock was oozing what felt like gallons of pre-cum.

"I wanna fuck that cute white ass of yours," he groaned in my ear. "I wanna stick my big ol' dick in that tight pussy and fuck the hell out of you till you spew cum all over me."

The thought of his plans sent both my mind and my body into spasms of excitement. Here was a real football player, and not something out of a magazine, wanting my ass and wanting to fuck it hard and solid. I had no fears that his size might split me because I had sent my mind into a fantasy world of raw sex. I wanted him to bend me over and slide his massive weapon into me and then let me ride him. In fact I wanted continuous sex; I didn't want him to stop, no matter how many times we both came.

Josh pulled out from between my legs and knelt in front of me, taking my cock into his warm mouth and slurping it down his throat. I could feel the tightness of pressure that he exerted on my shaft, almost making it feel as though he was trying to suck my cock and my balls down his throat and into his stomach. The friction on my cock was driving me crazy and I knew that if Josh didn't cool it, I was going to shoot my load.

"Be careful, Josh! You're getting me close!"

I suddenly felt a finger inserted into my tight little ass as he continued to suck. Now I was in trouble! There was no way I was going to be able to hold out.

"Aargh! Fuuck!" I shouted as I shot a heavy load down his thirsty throat. Josh swallowed as fast as I fired, load after load, and never did a drop escape his mouth. I fucked his face as I shot my load, groaning all the time, and as fast as I shot, so his finger manipulated my innards.

Slowly I began to come down from my 'high' but still he remained clamped to my cock, never allowing it to subside. Once he knew that I was ready for round two, he released my cock from his mouth and lay me down on the bed.

Josh walked over to his locker to get some condoms and lube. I watched as his smooth bubble-butt moved seductively and immediately my cock was completely back to life. He returned and unwrapped the condom foil.

He handed me the condom and said, "Roll it on white boy."

I was so excited by the prospect of him fucking me that my hands shook as I tried to get the sheer rubber over his massive length. I admired his glistening cock as he lubed it up and how the condom only reached three quarters down his length. He took a wad of lube and inserted two fingers into my ass, to loosen me up, then he knelt on the bed between my legs, hoisting them into the air and placing them on his broad, muscular shoulders. He took hold of my hips and dragged me closer to him, then taking hold of his thick shaft, he aimed at my entrance.

I felt the solid hardness of his cock head touch my opening and I tensed. Slowly he pushed forward in an effort to break through my sphincter. I could feel my opening being stretched as his bulbous, cut cock head forced its way through. The pain was intense, but I bore it bravely, determined not to disappoint my football man. More pressure was exerted until I gasped as his cock slid through the magic entrance and began a slow journey into my warm body, stretching and massaging my chute as he traveled. I gritted my teeth and held my breath as he entered me and Josh seemed to be doing likewise. At last, I felt his hips touch up against my ass cheeks and he remained still. We both exhaled and he smiled down at me.

"You've got a fuckin' tight ass, white kid. How's it feel to have this big black cock plugging that hole of your?"

I could only smile back as I tried to gain my breath and exclude the pain from my mind.

"Fucking awesome," I eventually managed to say.

Josh began pulling me further onto his long cock as he built up rhythmic thrusts deep into my chute and then sliding out until just the tip of his swollen cock head remained embedded in me. I gripped onto the back of his legs to pull him into me and between us we started thrusting against each other to gain deep penetration. I tightened the clasp on his shaft and Josh groaned as I did so, causing him to plow into my ass with gusto.

"Wrap your legs around my waist and your arms around my neck," insisted Josh.

I did as I was ordered and then felt his hands under each of my butt cheeks, spreading them wide and lifting me off the bed. He stood up with me still impaled on his solid cock and with my legs tightly wrapped around his waist for support. Using his arms, he started to lift me up and down on his cock while I hung on around his neck. In this manner, I could feel his cock go deep inside. I also felt as his hand supported my ass, that his fingers slid in alongside of his cock, creating more pressure for me. To have his thick cock as well as some fingers probing my ass, sent me into ecstasy.

Sweat was building up on his chest and brow and his thrusts were increasing in speed, until he suddenly stopped. I was worried that he'd had enough, but I was worrying unduly.

Josh lowered me back onto the bed and flipped me onto my side and lay down behind me. He spread my legs wide and continued plowing my ass, causing my body to vibrate with each thrust. He grabbed hold of my nipples and squeezed them, causing me to yelp, but at this stage, the pain I was enduring was more from pleasure than anything else.

Not content with our current position, Josh rolled onto his back, with me landing on top of him.

"Spin on my cock, white boy!"

Sitting on his cock, my back was to him, but he wanted me to turn to face him. As I rose and fell on his solid meat, so I turned myself around to face him.

"You wanted to ride this black stud's big cock, now do it!"

I rested the palms of my hands on the two pectoral mounds, letting my fingers pinch his nipples, and began to ride his massive weapon. My ass slid effortlessly over his long shaft, my butt cheeks smacking his balls each time I dropped down to the root of his cock. His groans were becoming more intense and the louder his groans became, the faster I rode him and the tighter I squeezed my ass muscles around his shaft.

"Fuck me white boy! Ride this fucking dick of mine! Harder! Feel this big black cock plow that tight chute of yours," he shouted.

I did as I was told and increased both my speed and tightness.

"Fuuuck!!" exclaimed Josh as he bucked skywards, taking me high into the air with him as he sank his meat deep into my warm chute and fired his first load.

I could feel his cock throbbing as it expelled each load, and, with the constant friction his cock had created in my chute, I too let loose with my load. Streams of white cum flowed onto his taut stomach and chest as an equal amount of hot, black man's cum flowed into me. As my cum sprayed across him, the contrast between the white cum and the brown skin was beautiful to see. I continued to clamp my ass and thighs tightly on Josh, milking every drop I could out of his throbbing cock until I lay exhausted across his stomach, spreading my white cum over both our bodies.

As we lay there, Josh stretched across to pick up his jock strap from the floor. Lovingly, he wiped us both clean with his jocks then held them up to my mouth. I sucked on them and smelt his manliness on the crotch. This in itself was a turn-on for me to sniff his jocks and for him to see me doing it, with the result that very soon we were back at it; my black football stud attacking my tight little white ass.

So good was our year together that Josh and I requested that we be room mates the following year at college and every time after that, whenever I heard the song 'Ebony and Ivory', my thoughts immediately flashed to Josh with his magnificent body and massive cock.

- MIDNIGHT COWBOY -

Ingredients:

2 oz Bourbon
1 oz Dark Rum
½ oz Heavy Cream

Directions:

In a shaker, half-filled with ice cubes, combine all the ingredients. Shake well and then strain into a cocktail glass.

BUCKING BRONCO

The horse was released from the starting pen with Joe on its back. It rushed into the arena, bucking and leaping in an effort to throw Joe from its back, but he held on tightly, flying into the air and crashing heavily back onto the horse's bare back. Joe's butt was snugly encased in his jeans, which fitted tightly over his muscular legs. Every time the horse bucked him into the air, body and jeans seemed to be glued to each other and flew into the air, and every time he returned to the horse's back, his butt and balls would slap against the flesh of the horse. The tightness of his jeans constricted any movement his cock or balls might normally have had, and every time he landed back on the horse, a warm sensation seemed to flood through his groin, up into his balls, and cause his cock to harden slightly. Joe's chief concern was to stay on the horse's back for as long as possible, so his attention was focused on this, rather than what was happening to his cock. However, his mind did slip for one brief moment, and Joe found himself flying through the air and landing rather heavily onto the dust ring. A rodeo hand ran to him to check that he was OK, but Joe was on his feet before the guy reached him. He dusted himself off, and as he did so, ran his hand over his hard-on in his jeans, trying to adjust the lie of his swollen cock.

Joe made his way to his trailer to go and relax.

"Good ride," shouted Bill, as Joe passed him near the announcer's booth. "How do you manage to stay on for so long?"

"I don't know," replied Joe.

"Have you got glue on those jeans of yours?" said Bill, as he walked with Joe towards Joe's trailer.

"Not that I'm aware of," said Joe. "Check if you like!"

Instinctively, Bill put a hand on Joe's tight ass and felt its firmness.

"There ain't any glue here, but this ass sure feels firm enough to clamp onto anything, including a horse's back," said Bill with a wry grin on his face.

"I just clamp these legs around the horse and hold on," replied Joe.

"That I can believe," stated Bill, "those legs are so strong, they could crush anything caught between them, including a horse," and he gave another wry smile to Joe.

Joe wouldn't admit it, but the way that Bill was talking and the way he placed his hand on Joe's ass, Joe could feel his hard-on growing.

Joe arrived at the door to his trailer. He opened the door and went up the steps into the coolness of its interior. Bill remained outside watching Joe's tight ass move smoothly into the trailer.

"Are you coming in?" shouted Joe from the interior of the trailer.

Bill ascended the steps and stood in the doorway. It was not the first time that he'd been in Joe's trailer, in fact whenever they were at the same rodeo he often went to Joe's trailer where the two guys would sit sharing stories and drinking the night away.

"Have a seat, Bill," shouted Joe from the kitchen area of the trailer.

Bill sat on a stool near the doorway and kicked the door of the trailer closed as he did so.

Joe came from the kitchen area carrying two beers, and Bill could see the bulge in the front of Joe's jeans. Joe crossed to Bill and handed him his beer. As he did so, Bill found himself face-to-face with Joe's bulge.

"Looking good," said Bill. "Looking big!"

Joe never moved, but remained standing in front of Bill with his legs apart, but firmly planted on the ground.

"Now how did you get that?" asked Bill, running a hand over the bulge in Joe's jeans.

"Riding that horse," replied Joe.

Bill laughed at Joe's reason. "You young guys don't even know how to ride a horse," said Bill, continuing to rub his hand over Joe's bulge.

"Do you reckon you older guys know any better," replied Joe, egging his mate on.

"I've been on this earth for the past forty-one years, so I think I know how to handle a bucking bronco, kid."

"Well, why don't you show me a thing or two, and let me decide whether you can handle a bucking bronco," said Joe, removing Bill's hands from his bulge and placing them firmly on his ass. "How do those two buns feel to you?"

"Hard like a horse's back," replied Bill, pulling Joe closer to him and placing his mouth on the denim covered bulge. His mouth followed the shape and length of Joe's hard-on over the denim of Joe's jeans. "Do you want to ride my horse?" asked Bill.

"I wouldn't mind getting my ass over that saddle of yours," replied Joe, bending down and feeling Bill's crotch. "It feels as if that saddle is quite hard," said Joe, licking his lips as he said it.

Joe lifted Bill to his feet and undid his jeans. As he did so, Bill unzipped Joe's. Joe had already kicked off his boots when he was in the kitchen. Bill slipped out of his jeans and shirt and returned to his seat, naked. Joe lay on the floor of the trailer and placed his feet on Bill's knees. Bill took hold of the bottoms of Joe's jeans and pulled. The jeans slid off Joe's hips and down his legs to his feet, revealing his large throbbing cock and his muscular legs. Bill stood up to get the jeans free from Joe's body, and as he did so, Joe's legs flipped into the air, revealing his tight little pink pucker.

Bill knelt on the floor between Joe's legs and began to rim Joe's ass. Joe's asshole quivered as Bill's tongue worked over its surface. Using his fingers, Bill gently prized open Joe's asshole and inserted his tongue. Joe groaned with ecstasy. Bill then moved his attention to Joe's balls and lathered them with his saliva. Slowly he worked his way up to Joe's massive dick. Bill licked the base and gently worked his way up its eight and a half inch length to wrap his mouth around the circumcised head. Joe was groaning for more, and Bill was obliging him by giving him the full works. Bill's mouth was experienced and he used it with expert effect. Joe was writhing on the floor and thrusting his cock deeply into Bill's throat. Bill wasn't going to end it so soon by making Joe shoot in his mouth. Instead, he was going to make this youngster of twenty-four, ride his dick like he would a bucking bronco.

Bill left Joe's cock and sat back on the stool. He leaned back and spread his legs wide apart. Joe rose to his knees and moved in between Bill's legs to start making love to Bill's fat dick. Although Bill's dick was a little shorter than Joe's, it was much thicker.

Joe opened his mouth as wide as he could and swallowed Bill's cock in one go, right down to its base. Bill grunted and groaned as Joe did this, and held tightly onto Joe's head so that he wouldn't release his grip on Bill's cock. Joe then slid his mouth to the tip of Bill's cock where he nibbled on Bill's foreskin. Joe continued his action on Bill's cock until Bill put his hands under Joe's arms and lifted him off the ground. As he did this, Joe held onto Bill's cock with his mouth, causing Bill's foreskin to stretch. Finally, Joe let go.

"Are you ready to ride this horse?" asked Bill.

"Sure," replied Joe, "but stand up."

Bill rose to his feet, not knowing what Joe had planned.

"Do you want to feel these legs?" asked Joe.

"Sure I do," said Bill.

Joe put his arms around Bill's neck and then leapt up, wrapping his legs around Bill's waist. Automatically, Bill grabbed Joe's buns to support him, and then he realized what Joe's plan was. Joe held on tightly with his strong legs while Bill parted Joe's buns. Joe could feel the tip of Bill's cock touch his asshole. The anticipation was getting too great for him. He released one hand from Bill's neck and held onto the base of Bill's dick, guiding it into his waiting ass. As he pushed down onto Bill's cock, Joe put his arm back around Bill's neck and forced his ass down on Bill's cock. Bill growled as his cock sank deeply into Joe's hot ass. Using his muscular legs, Joe began riding Bill's cock, slowly at first. He lifted his body up until Bill's cock was about to pop out of its hiding place, then Joe would force his body back down on Bill's length. This continued with both men groaning with pleasure and breathing heavily. Joe was doing all the work and could feel himself getting closer, so he stopped his action and climbed off Bill's cock.

"This horse is getting me close," he said, climbing from Bill.

"So is the horse," replied Bill, "because the rider is so good."

Bill sat down on the stool and spread his legs apart. Joe turned his back on Bill and lowered his ass onto Bill's dick. Joe could lean forward and look between his legs and see Bill's cock sliding in and out of his tight ass. Joe rode again, slowly, watching every entry and seeing every inch of Bill's thick cock disappearing into his ass. Bill's full length and width was buried in Joe and Joe ground his ass on Bill's cock. Bill cried out in absolute pleasure and thrust upwards, trying to bury his balls in Joe's ass as well.

"Oh Fuuuck!" cried Bill. "That feels sooo good! Ride my dick, kid. This is good!"

Joe increased his speed and found that by watching the movement as Bill's cock slid in and out of him, he was working himself up. He could feel himself nearing to explosion.

Bill's breathing had increased suddenly and his thrusts were that of a horse desperate to get rid of its rider. Joe bounced up and down on Bill's cock, frantically trying to milk it dry.

"Fuck me! Fuck this ass! Harder!!! Buck this ass!! It's waiting for your hot cum. Aargh!!" screamed Joe.

Sweat was pouring down his face and chest. If he could have got Bill's balls into his ass as well, he would have, he was riding so hard. Bill gave an almighty upward thrust and held it deep in Joe's ass.

"Aaaargh! Fuuuck!" he growled, pinching onto Joe's nipples and squeezing.

Both men fired their loads at the same time. Joe sent a spray up into the air, which landed on the floor and the following sprays went over him and Bill's legs. Bill, in the mean time was filling Joe with his hot cum. When both men were spent and Joe had squeezed his ass muscles to milk Bill of the last of his cum, Joe swiveled around on Bill's cock to face Bill.

"That was one studly horse I've just ridden," panted Joe.

"Fuck, that was one helluva rider that's just ridden this horse," replied Bill, wiping some sweat from his eyes.

Joe lifted his feet off the ground and wrapped his legs around Bill's waist and exerted pressure so that his legs pulled him further onto Bill's cock.

"Ohhhhh!" groaned Bill, as Joe did this. "Fuck it's so good when I'm inside of you."

"Well, do you think us young guys know how to ride?" asked Joe.

"I think you're good," said Bill, "but I think I'll have to give you some more lessons, if that's OK with you?"

"This ass is always available for a good fuck, and any time you want to be a bucking bronco, this rider's ready for you," quipped Joe, still clenching onto Bill's waist with his strong legs.

Every now and again, Joe would tense his legs around Bill's waist, causing Bill's still erect cock to stay deep in Joe's ass. Joe actually noticed that by doing this he was able to keep Bill hard for a very long time, so long in fact that he soon felt Bill begin to give his ass some upward thrusts again, and soon the two men were practicing their riding techniques again.

An hour later, Bill and Joe got dressed, Joe pouring his body into his tight jeans and the two of them left the confines of the trailer and headed back to the rodeo arena, where both of them were to ride again, but this time it was on horses.

"How about us having a wager?" said Bill.

"What did you have in mind?" asked Joe.

"You reckon you younger riders are better than us older ones. Well if you beat me, you get to pound my ass, but if I beat you, you ride this bucking bronco. Deal?"

Joe thought about it for a moment, and then replied, "Agreed. Deal."

A number of rodeo riders were to appear first in the arena before Bill or Joe was to appear. They did their best to stay on their horses and their times varied.

"The next competitor to ride is Joe Ashkansky," announced the announcer.

Joe readied himself above the horse at the entry gate. He locked his gloved hand into the support rope.

"Ready!" said Joe.

The gate flung open and Joe and his horse reared into the arena. Joe was being bounced up and down on the horse's back, and once again, the sensation that he was beginning to feel between his legs was gratifying. The bouncing warmed his ass and again the feeling traveled through his balls and up the shaft of his cock, until it was once again erect. He could feel it pressing tightly against the denim of his jeans and he had visions of shooting his load while he was on the horse. He could feel himself begin to slide sideways. He was going to fall. He tried to right himself, but it was too late. Joe slid to the ground and protected himself from the flying hooves of the horse.

"Twenty three seconds," shouted the announcer. "We've got a new leader."

The crowd roared their approval and Joe picked himself up from the dust. He walked over to the starting gate to wait for Bill's ride. Bill was standing there smiling as Joe neared him.

"That was a damn good time, but I see that ass of yours let you down again."

"What do you mean?" asked Joe.

"Just look at that bulge in those jeans. I thought I'd milked you dry of everything, but obviously I was wrong."

Joe looked down at the bulge in the front of his jeans, and then looked sheepishly at Bill.

"I told you I liked getting my ass worked," said Joe.

The announcer called out Bill's name and he climbed onto the side fence and straddled the horse's back.

"Just imagine you're straddling me," joked Joe.

"Forget it buddy that cock of yours ain't going near this ass of mine."

"Ready," said Bill, and the gate opened.

The horse leapt into the arena with Bill bouncing on its back. He fought to keep his balance while the horse tried to get rid of its passenger. The more the horse tried, the more Bill held on. Joe stood watching the clock tick by as Bill fought to stay on.

Eighteen seconds! Bill was looking a little tired. Too much sex thought Joe!

Twenty seconds, and still Bill is on the horse. Twenty-four seconds! Bill knows that his ass is safe, but Joe's is not. Joe smiles when he realizes this and rubs his hands over his tight butt. Twenty-eight seconds and Bill is now lying in the dust. He jumps to his feet as the crowd goes wild. He runs over to where Joe is standing and leaps over the railings.

"Not bad for an old guy, eh? And what's even better is I get to taste that sexy ass again."

Joe patted Bill on the back and congratulated him on a good performance.

"A deal is a deal," said Joe. "And this ass is yours," he continued, turning to show his tight ass to Bill.

Bill laughed when he saw this, licked his lips and added, "When do I get it?"

"As the event's over, you get to eat it now. My trailer or yours?"

"I like it when you ride this stud in your trailer," replied Bill.

The two men, one young and the other younger, headed off in the direction of Joe's trailer, but anyone watching them could see that the young man walked slightly behind the younger man, and watched the gentle sway of the younger man's hips as the younger man's buns were held tightly in their denim protection. At the door to the trailer, the younger man turned his head to face the young man and rubbed both hands over his butt.

"OK Stud, this ass is going to bust your balls for you," said Joe, opening the door and going into the trailer while Bill followed, unzipping his jeans as he did so.

When they were undressed, Joe spread himself out on his back on the sofa-cum-bed, like someone waiting to be sacrificed. Bill stood at the bottom of the bed, his thick uncut dick rising to the occasion. He moved in closer to Joe and proceeded to lick his way up the length of Joe's muscular legs. As he neared Joe's crotch, Bill's hand moved in under Joe's tight ass and began to search for an entry. Joe automatically raised his legs into the air and Bill saturated Joe's balls with saliva. His tongue worked its way under his balls, heading for the opening in Joe's ass. When Bill saw Joe's pucker wink at him, he spat into it and rubbed a finger over it, inserting it ever so slightly. Joe groaned as he felt Bill's finger touch his magic spot. Bill ran two fingers over the area and gently inserted them. This action slowly increased until he had four fingers firmly inserted in Joe's ass. He spread his fingers, opening Joe's asshole wider. Joe was writhing in ecstasy and growling as Bill continued sending Joe on a fantastic trip. Bill wrapped his lips around Joe's cock, which was already oozing pre-cum from its tip. When Bill's mouth touched Joe's cock, it was ready to explode.

"Aargh! Fuck me before I shoot all over the place," groaned Joe.

"Do you like this?" whispered Bill.

"Oh yes, stud. I want that cock of yours. Push it in, for fuck sake!"

"Not yet my young rider, I want you to enjoy the ride."

Bill pushed his fingers a little deeper into Joe.

"Aargh fuck, I'm coming!" shouted Joe, and shot a wad of hot cum over his stomach.

Immediately his ass clamped around Bill's fingers, but Bill didn't stop spreading them. He gently continued to move then in and out of Joe's throbbing asshole, while Joe shot load after load.

"I like that," said Bill, rubbing Joe's hot cum over his stomach and chest where it had landed.

Bill's own cock was beginning to discharge some pre-cum as he watched Joe's ass throb gently.

Slowly Bill withdrew his fingers, then inserted them again, and withdrew them and inserted them. He continued this action getting Joe worked up again.

"I'm going to make you come again, kid," said Bill. "Remember you said you were going to bust my balls. Show me that this young rider can do it."

Bill moved his body closer to Joe's, slid his hand out of Joe's asshole and moved his swollen cock in to position to take the place of his fingers. He aimed his cock at Joe's entry, lifted Joe's legs high into the air and ravaged that tight ass of Joe's. Bill plunged into the opening. Joe had been loosened up, so he felt no pain; in any case he was too filled with pleasurable feelings to worry about any possible pain. Bill pounded into Joe's ass.

"I want that dick of yours," said Joe. "Let go of my legs."

Bill did so and immediately Joe wrapped his strong legs around Bill's waist, pulling Bill's cock deeper into his ass. Joe's ass was lifted off the bed and he held it high in the air while his shoulders acted as his support. With his hands now free, Bill took hold of Joe's cock and started stroking it. Joe was grunting as he thrust his ass onto Bill's length. Bill's dick kept rubbing against Joe's prostate causing him immense pleasure.

"Ah, fucking hell this is great! Eat my ass! Fuck it harder, stud. Make me come, you fucker! Ah yes!" screamed Joe.

"Fuuuck! I'm coming," shouted Bill.

"Pump me baby! Fuck this ass!" cried Joe, clamping his sphincter tightly around Bill's dick. "Fucker, you're making shoot my load again!"

Both men exploded their juices at the same time. Both of them pounded into each other, until Joe thought his ass was going to split and Bill's balls began to ache.

Bill's breathing was heavy and he felt dizzy from the excitement he had experienced. Joe had a warm, tingling feeling running through his body.

"Don't take it out yet," said Joe. "I want to fell it inside me a little longer."

"Don't worry," panted Bill, "you'll feel this inside you as long as you want to and whenever you want to. You know, for a kid, you sure know how to bust a man's balls and work on his dick. I think that tight ass of yours has strangled this dick of mine. In fact I think that tight ass of yours is just as tight around my dick as your mouth was."

As Bill's dick slipped from Joe, he let go of his crushing leg grip around Bill's waist and dropped his legs onto the bed. Bill lay on top of Joe and moved his body over Joe's so that he could rub Joe's warm cum over both of them.

Joe laughed, "You know for an old fucker, you're not bad."

"Old!" exclaimed Bill, "and not bad! I'm bloody good."

"No you're not," said Joe, "you're fucking good! And this ass of mine can't get enough of the fat dick of yours, so when's the next rodeo?"

"Why wait for the next rodeo. How about tonight?"

Joe just laughed. "You really want to fuck the hell out of me."

"That's the problem with you youngsters, you can't take the pace!" smiled Bill, and the two lay in each other's arms until they both fell asleep.

- **BMW** -

Ingredients:

⅓ oz Bailey's Irish Cream
⅓ oz Malibu Rum
⅓ oz White Crème de Cacao

Directions:

Shake all the ingredients together with ice and strain into a shot glass.

BROTHERLY LOVE

Gary and Tony had grown up in a middle-class family background, the only children of a working father and home-keeping mother. This family had nothing out of the ordinary about it; suffice to say that when the two boys grew up and left school, they said they wanted to become cops. There was nothing disgraceful about becoming a policeman, except that their mother wasn't too keen because of the element of danger involved. Up until this time, no one in the family had ever considered the police force as a career and quite where this idea came from, bewildered both their parents.

Gary, at twenty-three, was two years older than Tony and apart from an age difference, their looks and personalities also differed. Tony, tall, fair, with an athletic build, tended to be the quieter or more reserved of the two, or so their parents said. Gary, on the other hand, was more stocky, with a dark moustache, and seemed always to be in trouble, whether he went looking for it or whether it merely found him, one didn't know. However, Gary had always had a caring nature about him and he always supported and defended his 'baby' brother if he ever got into trouble, which wasn't that often.

After Gary had completed his schooling, he had worked for a while on a construction site until Tony had finished school and then the two of them enlisted in the police force. Growing up they had led pretty separate lives, but now that they were together in the police, they tended to become closer. Once they had finished their initial training, they applied to join the motorcycle section, as they both had a passion for motorbikes. They had no problem being accepted into the bike section as they both had tremendous skills for riding and they knew they were good at it.

On the first day of duty, their mother was proud of her two boys who were smartly turned out in their blue uniforms, looking handsome.

"I'm so proud of you," she said, hugging both of them at the same time, "but I still worry about your safety."

"Don't worry, Mum," replied Gary, "we'll be just fine, you'll see."

"Please keep an eye on your baby brother here," she continued.

"Ah Mum, as Gary says, we'll be fine. You don't have to worry about us; we'll keep an eye on each other. In fact I won't let Gary out of my sight."

"I hope that doesn't include when I go to the toilet?"

"You bet, I'll be there to see you don't come to any harm," laughed Tony.

The boys straddled their motorbikes, started them up and sped off in the direction of their police station. The wind blew into their faces and they felt an element of freedom to be out on the road. They soon arrived at the station and reported for duty. The officer in charge decided it would be better for the two of them to split up so that they could work with a different partner until they were accustomed to how things were done. Gary was paired with a chap by the name of Doug who was slightly older than him, built like an ox and who also sported a moustache, while Tony was placed with Mike, a thirty-something with short cropped blonde hair and the physique of a gymnast.

Tony and Mike left after they had been given their morning instructions and headed out into the country. After about fifteen minutes of riding, they pulled to the side of the road and parked their bikes.

"How long have you been in the force, Mike?"

"I think it's coming up for about ten years," he replied.

"And how long have you been on bikes then?"

"That's been about six years, but I wouldn't change it for anything. It's great to be able to get out into the open air and not be stuck behind a desk in an office. You've got more freedom here."

"Yes, I think that's why I opted for it, so that I could have the freedom."

"Was that your brother with you?"

"Mm! He's also started in the bike section today, but he's older than I am and he waited until I'd finished school and then we joined the force together."

"Are you married, Tony?"

"No, nothing as serious as that yet. I want to enjoy my life before somebody gets their claws into me. Are you married?"

"I was, but thank goodness that's over with now. We actually weren't made for each other, so perhaps it was better that we broke up. At least there weren't any children to feel the suffering and pain."

"Well that's one consolation. It's always a pity when that sort of thing happens. So often it's the children who get overlooked and it's their emotions that suffer."

"Are you going out with someone?" asked Mike.

"No, I'm a bit of a loner, not that it means I don't like going out, because I do. What about yourself?"

"I just go out with the boys occasionally" replied Mike, with a tinge of sadness that filtered through his voice as he said it.

"Well maybe we can go for a drink some time," said Tony, trying to brighten up the situation.

"Actually, that would be nice. I think I'd like that. Particularly if we're going to be riding together, I ought to get to know you better."

Meanwhile, Gary and Doug had also gone out into the country area and had parked at the side of the road to watch the traffic. The only difference in the conversations that were taking place here, as opposed to Tony and Mike's, was that Gary and Doug sounded and looked like two peacocks competing against each other. They both sat astride their motorbikes, preening themselves in the wing mirrors, stroking their moustaches as if they were trying to stretch them further out towards their ears.

"Have you been going to the gym?" asked Gary as he surveyed Doug's bulky frame.

"I used to go quite regularly, but I find I haven't got time now, so I only go when it's possible, which isn't that often. What about yourself?"

"Same with me. I used to but then it became a mission to make the effort, so I stopped."

"You must be careful because when you stop, the muscle can turn to fat and that's not so good."

"Don't worry," replied Gary, "I've got no intentions of getting to that stage. I pride my body."

"Was that your brother that came with you this morning?"

"Mm. He's a bit younger than me, but he's a good kid."

"He also looks like he's got a good body on him too. Does he go to gym?"

"I think he went for a while, but then gave it up; but he's got one of those naturally well developed bodies. You know there's always one who's born with such luck."

The conversation stopped there and both looked in their side mirrors to preen themselves once more.

The day continued pretty uneventfully for Tony and Gary, and at the end of their shift they sped home on their bikes. It had been agreed upon that when they started in the police force they were going to move out of their parent's house and move into their own, which they were going to share. After pausing to say "hi" to their parents and let them know how the first day had gone, the boys continued home. When they arrived home, they parked their bikes and grabbed a beer each from the fridge and settled down in front of the TV.

"What was your day like, Gary?'

"Nothing exciting happened. Just sat most of the day by the side of the road, checking the traffic."

Tony roared with laughter. "Same here. If that's what it's going to be like, I think I'm going to quit now before it gets even more boring."

"Hey, I don't think you should give in so easily. I thought you were a fighter?"

"Don't take me seriously. Of course I'm not going to quit. In any case I think my partner's OK."

"What do you mean by OK?"

"He seems a cool guy, but built like a brick shithouse. I wouldn't mess with him."

"I like my partner as well. He said that he was married, but he's divorced now, but he seems quite a decent sort. Actually, I think that they've paired us up quite well; you with your brick shithouse and me with my quiet, gentle sort of guy."

"Are you implying that I'm like a shithouse?" roared Gary with laughter.

"Not at all, but you're big like him, that's what I meant."

The two brothers continued to talk about their first day like two excited school children might do after their first day at school, but most of all, they enjoyed their work.

The days went into weeks and Gary and Tony were like old hands on their bikes; equally, their friendships with Mike and Doug grew stronger and the feeling of trust developed between each partner. After they had been in the bike section for a month, Gary suggested that they invite Doug and Mike around for dinner.

"Who's cooking?" asked Gary.

"We're both going to cook and you're not getting out of this meal."

Doug and Mike agreed to the dinner date, and on the selected evening, the four men got together at Gary and Tony's place. The food was good and the drinks flowed. The conversation was animated and the company was scintillating. Tony felt a strange affiliation to Mike as though he was becoming attracted to him, but he thought that it might just be the fact that they were partners.

As the drinks flowed, so the conversation changed from one topic to another until it reached the inevitable subject of sex.

"Mike tells me that you haven't got a girlfriend, Tony," said Doug, but without any venom in his tone.

"That's right," Tony replied.

"Why not? You're a good looking guy who could catch any woman."

"I don't know," replied Tony, "I just haven't really given it much thought."

"Are you a fagot, then?" said Doug roaring with laughter at what he had just said.

Tony felt a little embarrassed and Gary wasn't quite sure how to take that statement.

"I have got a few friends who are gay and I like their company, but does that worry you?"

"Not at all. It's just that you don't have a girl, and I wondered."

Gary thought he ought to change the subject, but before he could, Mike spoke up.

"Even if he is gay, what difference does it make? I'm his partner and I have to work with him and I trust him, which is the most important aspect. If you can't trust your partner, then you can't trust anybody."

"I agree with Mike," retorted Gary, feeling a little more at ease now that Mike had spoken up in Tony's defense.

Doug didn't respond, but merely smirked. Nothing more was said about the possibility of Tony's sexuality, but it did seem to place a damper on the evening and very soon Mike said that he thought it was time for him to go. Doug, however, continued to sit, until Mike suggested that they leave together as neither of them was very sober and they could help each other home. They thanked Gary and Tony for the evening and departed, leaving Tony piling the plates into the sink and washing up. After Gary had seen them out, he returned to the kitchen to help his brother clean up. Tony was at the sink when Gary entered the kitchen. He walked up behind Tony and put his arms around his shoulder.

"Thanks for a brilliant evening, baby brother. I really enjoyed myself and I hope that you did too."

Tony didn't react, but continued to wash up.

"Listen, don't take what Doug said too seriously. It's probably the beer talking, and in any case, even if you are gay, so what, you're still my brother."

Still Tony never said anything. It was almost as if he had been hurt. Gary gave him a squeeze and nuzzled into Tony's neck. Tony could feel the bulge in his brother's crotch pressing up against his ass and it gave him a tingling sensation. He knew that he was gay and that the feeling he was encountering from his brother was exciting to him, but his brother had no idea of his feelings. His mind was racing. Should he tell Gary of his lifestyle and feelings or should he just keep it to himself. So often this was the problem with many young men; they couldn't tell anyone for fear of rejection and recriminations. He could feel his own bulge beginning to grow in the front of his jeans from the touch he was receiving from his brother. He turned to face Gary and putting his arms around Gary's neck, he hugged him. He didn't care if Gary felt his hard-on.

"Thanks Gary, I really appreciate you being here."

Gary looked into his baby brother's eyes and lowered his hand to where their crotches were touching.

"What's this?" Gary asked as he felt the bulge in Tony's jeans. "Are you gay or is this from the drink?"

Tony wasn't sure which answer to offer, but instead chose to break away from their embrace and go back to the washing up.

"Put it down to the drink if you like," he said putting more plates into the sink.

Gary backed away, then turned and went into the lounge where he put some music on the CD player. Tony felt his erection subsiding after Gary's departure, but he wondered what was going through his brother's mind.

After he had completed the washing and drying, he also went into the lounge and sat down to listen to the music. Gary was sprawled out on the couch with his eyes closed, listening to the music.

"What did you think of Mike?" asked Tony.

"He seems quite a decent sort of bloke, and I think you'll get on well with him," replied Gary, stroking his moustache, "but I can't actually understand how he and Doug seem to get on so well. They seem complete opposites."

"I suppose it's just that they've been working together for so long," muttered Tony.

"Tell me, did Doug really upset you when he asked you if you were gay?"

"It's just that I didn't expect it from him. I was probably more surprised than anything else," answered Tony.

"But you're not are you?"

Tony didn't answer but merely stretched out and started to hum in time to the music, pretending that he hadn't heard what Gary had asked.

"Hey! I'm talking to you!" shouted Gary above the sound of the music and the humming.

"Sorry, what did you say?"

"I asked you if you were gay."

"Well now, that would be for me to know and for you to find out," laughed Tony standing up from his seat. "I think I'm going to bed. Good night big brother, see you in the morning." Tony left Gary in the lounge and made his way to his bedroom.

Gary's mind, in the mean time, began to think about the evening's happenings. If his brother was gay, there was nothing that he could do about it, but where would that put him with regard to work and his workmates. The other officers would start talking and he would have to listen to the things that they might say about Tony and he wasn't sure how he would be able to handle these situations. Eventually, Gary fell asleep on the couch and stayed there until Tony woke him in the early morning in order to get up and get ready for work.

At work that day, nothing much was said of the previous evening, except Mike made a point of thanking both Gary and Tony for the enjoyable evening.

"I'm glad that you enjoyed yourself," said Tony, "because I was glad that you could come for dinner."

"I'm sorry about the way Doug behaved, but you've got to excuse him; when he's had a few drinks he often doesn't realize what he says or does, but he's really quite harmless."

Although Mike and Tony seemed to chat together quite freely, Gary didn't seem to join in much.

After their morning briefings were over, the men mounted their bikes and set off, Tony and Mike going in one direction, while Doug and Gary set off in another. Doug set off in the direction of the highway with Gary following and they continued in this fashion for at least 30 miles until Doug pulled off at the side of the road near to a bridge. When Gary saw this, he too pulled off and parked his bike next to Doug's. They sat astride their bikes, neither speaking. Eventually, Gary spoke.

"I hope you enjoyed yourself last night, Doug?"

"It was great thanks."

"Did you two guys go straight back home after you left us, or did you go out for more drinks?"

"Mike went home, but I went to a pub for a few more, then I went home," replied Doug curtly.

"Did you score anything?" asked Gary.

"What's that supposed to mean?" retorted Doug, straightening himself up on his bike.

"I merely wondered whether you managed to pick someone up for the night!"

"No!" was the abrupt answer.

Just then over the radio came an announcement that a yellow BMW convertible was racing in their direction and they had to stop it and charge the driver with speeding. Doug alighted from his bike and moved to the edge of the road in anticipation of the speeding BMW. There were not many cars passing along this section of the road and it was fairly flat and open so they could see when a car was approaching. Soon a bright yellow vehicle was spotted heading towards them. Doug moved into the middle of the road in order to flag the driver down and Gary joined him at the side of the road. As the driver approached, he began to slow down when he saw the two officers in the road. Doug waved his arms to tell the driver to pull over to the side of the road, which he did and both Doug and Gary moved closer to the car. Gary moved to the passenger's side while Doug made for the driver's side.

When they reached the car, which had its roof down and which contained only a driver, they looked at him; he was no older than twenty, but old enough to have a driver's license. He had short, blonde hair, deep blue eyes and was wearing a T-shirt spread tightly over his upper torso and a pair of Lycra running shorts.

"Good day officers, what seems to be the trouble?"

"You are," glowered Doug, as he sized up the young man and the motorcar. "You've been speeding."

"I'm sorry about that," he replied, "but it's difficult to keep this car from going slowly."

"Is this your car?" asked Gary, walking around it to survey it.

"Yes, my parents bought it for me last Christmas."

"Spoilt brat," muttered Doug under his breath. "And what's the hurry, then?"

"No hurry," replied the young man, smiling at both officers.

"Get out of the car!" blurted Doug.

The young man opened the door and stretched his long, athletic legs out of the car and stood up. He was about the same height as both Doug and Gary, but had a streamlined body that was well suited to his tight T-shirt and Lycra gym shorts.

Doug eyed him up and down; then walked to where Gary was and said, "I hate these young spoilt brats. They need to be taught a lesson."

Doug walked back to the young man.

"Lean on the bonnet and spread your legs," commanded Doug.

"But I've done nothing wrong," pleaded the young man.

"Just do as you are told," boomed Doug's voice.

The young man became a little apprehensive when he heard the booming voice and positioned himself over the bonnet and spread his legs as he had been told to do. Doug moved in behind the young man and ran his hands down his back, as though feeling for concealed weapons. His hands then moved to the front and ran over the man's chest and through the tightness of the T-shirt; Doug felt the hardness of the young man's nipples. His hands then trailed to the man's hips and butt. Doug felt the smooth bubble-butt and also felt it tense as the young man tensed his body. Doug lowered himself into a crouching position as he felt up and down each leg, which was quite the silliest of things to do as the young man wasn't wearing long trousers and so couldn't conceal anything on his legs. Doug's hands moved into the inner thigh area and up between the young man's balls. Doug felt their firmness and the growing bulge that lay encased in the front of the Lycra shorts. For a moment, he let his hand lie there enjoying the gentle pulsing of the young man's cock as it throbbed and grew. Doug then stood up and commanded the young man to turn around and face him. When the man did so, his face was flushed and Doug could plainly see that the young man was extremely well endowed, but Gary was standing there watching, so he couldn't do anything about it if he had wanted to.

"I'm going to have to give you a ticket for speeding," said Doug, eyeing the man up and down, but having lowered the volume of his voice as he said it. "What is your name and address and phone number?"

"Marc Skatch," replied the young man, smiling at Doug. "62 Brakley Road, telephone 7146008, and I live alone," he continued, quietly so that Gary didn't hear him.

Doug returned the smile and made a note of the information. He also scribbled something on a piece of paper and handed it to Marc.

"That's your ticket and don't let us catch you speeding again," said Doug loudly. "Now be on your way."

Gary went back to his motorbike. As Marc got back into his car, he looked at the piece of paper Doug had given him and saw that it was Doug's telephone number and name, and that he hadn't been given a fine. Marc smiled back at the big man, who was standing alongside the car, and rubbed his hand over his extremely swollen crotch as if to taunt Doug.

"Phone me," whispered Doug, and the car sped off.

"How much did you fine him?" shouted Gary as the car sped away.

"I gave him a written warning instead and told him to behave and drive like an adult and not like some spoilt little brat."

Three days later Doug received a phone call from Marc, inviting him around for a drink after work. His mind flashed back to the day he and Gary stopped Marc and remembered the lithe athletic body with the large package in the crotch area, and as he thought about it, he felt the sudden tingling urge between his legs as his dick began to swell. After work, he made his way home, showered, dressed in his leather jeans and jacket and then climbed back onto his bike and rode around to Marc's house.

The doorbell chimed and soon the door was opened by Marc, looking refreshed and cool in a tight pair of jeans and a white vest, which showed off his pectorals and biceps to advantage. Doug stood staring at Marc for a moment, admiring what he saw.

"Gee, you look good," stammered Doug, letting his eyes follow the length of Marc's frame.

"Thanks, so do you," replied Marc. "Are you going to stand there staring or are you coming in?"

"Thanks. Oh, is it OK if I leave my bike there in the drive?"

"Sure, but you're welcome to put it in the garage, if you'd prefer," answered Marc. "Actually, it might be safer there. I'll open up for you," he continued.

Marc led Doug to the garage, opened the door and he pushed his bike into the area next to the BMW. Doug stood admiring the yellow BMW while Marc closed the garage door again.

"Do you like it?" asked Marc walking up to Doug at the car.

"I wouldn't mind handling that," replied Doug, running a hand over the sleek yellow body of the BMW.

"Is that all you'd mind handling?" enquired Marc, with a slight grin on his face.

At first Doug wasn't quite sure what he had heard, but when he looked at Marc's smile and the way he was dressed, he realized what Marc had said.

"It's funny, but I quite fancy your bike, you know," said Marc strolling over to Doug's bike and straddling it. He felt the smoothness of the leather seat rub between his legs as they were stretched wide.

"Are you into bikes?" asked Doug, moving over to where Marc was seated.

"I think they're quite a turn-on," replied Marc, as he held onto the handlebars, pretending to ride.

Marc leaned forward and rested his chest across the petrol tank as though to imitate a racing position, and while he was in that position, Doug climbed onto the seat behind Marc and pushed his crotch close up against Marc's ass. Marc felt the pressure against him, but didn't move away. Doug leaned against Marc's back and put his arms around him so as to hold onto the handlebars. Marc immediately felt protected by the big, burly policeman. Marc pushed back slightly and felt the growing urgency in Doug's leathers.

They stayed like this for a moment and then Doug let go of the handlebars and put his arms around Marc's waist, but only for a short while because they soon found their way up Marc's vest to those firm, round nipples that were seeking attention. He cupped his hands over Marc's pecs and squeezed them, then let his fingers pinch each nipple gently. Marc released a soft groan when he felt this and pushed back harder against Doug.

"Do you want to go inside?" whispered Marc.

"No, I'd like to take you here," whispered Doug into Marc's ear.

Doug alighted from the bike and undid his shirt, revealing a well-developed upper body with a thin layering of dark hair covering his chest. He threw his shirt onto the floor and stood there rubbing a hand over his large round nipples and squeezing them hard. Marc threw a leg over the bike so he was now leaning on it and slowly pulled his vest over his head to reveal his smooth body. Doug advanced towards Marc and placed both hands over his young friend's pecs and then bent down to kiss each nipple, allowing his tongue to play with them. His tongue continued its journey in a southerly direction until it reached Marc's crotch where it lingered for a moment, moving up and down the length of Marc's swollen cock. Doug then removed his mouth and began to unzip Marc's jeans. As the zip moved down, so Marc's large cock flopped from its hideaway and Doug smiled in wonder at its beauty. His mouth didn't hesitate in taking his newfound joy into its warm cavity. His tongue and lips worked the full length of Marc's cock, giving both of them absolute pleasure. Marc merely threw his head back and groaned with pleasure.

"Ah, that feels good," sighed Marc.

For some time, Doug worked on Marc's thick cock, lathering it with his tongue. Eventually he removed his mouth from Marc's length and proceeded to disrobe Marc of his jeans. When Marc was standing naked in front of him, he admired the taut smooth body of the young man.

"Get on the bike," said Doug, with a smile on his face.

Marc went to mount the bike, but Doug stopped him.

"I want you to sit astride the bike, but face the back and not the front of the bike."

Marc smiled to himself and then mounted the bike in the position that Doug had requested, stretching his back across the petrol tank.

Doug undid his leather jacket and removed it to reveal a bulky, hairy chest with good definition. He threw his jacket onto the car that stood nearby and unbuttoned his leather jeans. As he slowly unbuttoned them the thickness of his cock emerged and Marc smiled. Although Marc's cock was longer than Doug's, not by much, Doug's was much thicker than Marc's.

Doug moved up to the bike and, climbing on, straddled Marc's body until his cock was situated over Marc's mouth. Marc opened his mouth and, holding Doug's erection, he directed it into the depths of his throat, where he began to make love to its thickness. His tongue worked under Doug's foreskin and then his mouth forced the foreskin to slide all the way back to reveal a purplish, mushroom-shaped head. Doug thrust forward when Marc did this. After some time, Doug pulled out of Marc's mouth and positioned himself at the rear of the bike and, lifting Marc's legs into the air, proceeded to rim Marc.

Once Doug had loosened Marc's ass muscles, he picked up a condom from his jacket pocket, unrolled it onto his length, held his dick at its base, aimed at Marc's asshole and slowly began to penetrate into the warm depths of Marc. Marc gasped as Doug's cock sank deeper, stretching him, until he felt Doug's balls resting against his ass.

"Oh that feels so good," moaned Marc. "Fuck me hard!"

Doug needed no request, as it was his intention to do just that, because ever since he had stopped Marc on the road and had seen his body and bulging crotch, he had been determined to get it.

"I want that ass of yours," groaned Doug as he ploughed in and out of Marc's ass as it tensed and relaxed to meet every thrust from Doug.

With each thrust from Doug, Marc's legs were flung back in the air and a groan or grunt was emitted each time, but throughout this, Marc kept a contented smile on his face.

Doug grasped onto Marc's shoulders for support and, holding him tightly, increased his rhythm and leant forward to bite onto Marc's lips. Their mouths clamped to each other's like magnets and Doug sucked hard on Marc's tongue, almost swallowing it down his throat. When he eventually released it, Marc gasped and met Doug's thrusts with intensified urgency. Marc could feel the girth of Doug's cock increasing, as did his breathing.

"Are you getting close?" gasped Marc.

"Oh fuck, this is great, and you're so tight. I'm going to come if you carry on like this," groaned Doug, sweat trickling from his face and body.

Marc stopped thrusting onto Doug's cock and relaxed a little so that his ass muscles didn't clamp so tightly around Doug's dick. He smiled at Doug and slowly pulled off Doug's cock. Doug wondered what Marc was planning and was a little concerned because he was getting close and didn't want to be left on a high and not come, but Marc wasn't about to let his guest down. Marc climbed from the bike and turning to face the front of it, re-mounted it so he was facing the petrol tank. Doug slid closer to Marc and Marc, taking hold of Doug's cock, guided it back into his pleasure-zone. He leant forward onto the tank and raised his ass, allowing Doug to attack it once more. They continued in this position for some time until Marc shouted that he was nearing the edge of no return. Doug immediately thrust more deeply making Marc's hard cock slide across part of the leather seat and part of the petrol tank. The smoothness of both surfaces was creating a friction, which was exciting to Marc.

"I'm coming!" exclaimed Marc, pushing back onto Doug's already throbbing cock, and as Marc fired the first of his powerful loads across the petrol tank, so his ass muscles clamped once more around Doug's thick cock and he felt the warmness exploding inside of him. When they had exhausted their supplies, Marc collapsed across the wet, sticky petrol tank while Doug lay across Marc's back, kissing his neck and thanking him for the pleasure that he had received. After recovering their breath, Doug slowly pulled out of Marc, leaving him with a sense of emptiness and dismounted from the bike. Marc then also dismounted and with a rather sheepish smile, said, "I'm sorry about the mess on your bike."

"Hey don't worry about that; I want that as a souvenir," answered Doug, with a slap on Marc's shoulders.

That evening, the two men enjoyed each other's company more than once.

————————

The following day, when Doug and Gary went out on their patrols, they chatted about the usual things like what they had done the previous night and what was planned for them for the day. Doug never said anything about his experience with Marc, but soon they decided to park off the side of the road for a rest. As they were sitting on their bikes, casually watching the passing motorists, Gary noticed the marks on Doug's bike.

"Hey, that bike of yours looks pretty dirty on the tank there," said Gary, pointing to the marks.

Doug seemed a little embarrassed and tried to cover up for it.

"Were you out with someone last night, you horny bastard?" laughed Gary.

"You could say that," replied Doug, still a little hesitant about sharing the information.

"Well, you sure made a mess coming all over the bike like that, if that is cum there."

Doug merely grunted something, which Gary didn't fully hear.

"Was she good?" continued Gary.

"Great," came back the reply.

"So what's her name?"

"I don't know," said Doug, now beginning to try to avoid the subject.

"You mean it was just wham bam thank you ma'am, plough it in and pull it out!" said a surprised Gary.

"Not really, it's just that we were so involved I didn't bother to ask her name or number."

"Well if you didn't do that, then she couldn't have been that great," smiled Gary.

"No she was; it's just that we were both in a hurry."

Doug realized that he was getting himself into more trouble, the more he continued this conversation, so he changed it and spoke about the previous night's football games.

Doug and Gary sat for quite some time at the side of the road under the shade of a willow tree. While they were sitting on their bikes, Gary suddenly said, "Hey, check this out; here comes that guy in his yellow BMW that we stopped."

Doug froze where he was, hoping that Marc wouldn't see them in the shadows of the tree, but unfortunately he was alert and spotted them. As he neared the two police officers, he slowed down and as he came alongside them, he stopped.

"Hi guys, are you two having a smoke break or were you waiting to catch me again?"

Gary laughed and waved, but Doug continued to look embarrassed.

"Hey Doug, thanks again for last night," shouted Marc, "anytime you feel like coming round, you're more than welcome," and he revved up the car and drove off.

Gary looked quizzically at Doug, who tried to avoid eye contact with Gary.

"What did he mean by that?" Gary asked.

"Oh I just saw him for a while last night," replied Doug rather sheepishly.

"Was that before or after you had your quickie?" joked Gary.

"Why all the interrogation?" said Doug, now shifting uneasily on his bike.

Gary thought for a while, then his eye seemed to widen.

"Don't tell me you did! He said that he was with you last night. Did something happen? I mean … the marks on your bike – is that your cum or someone else's?"

"What difference does it make whose fucking cum it is; it's got nothing to do with you."

"No, you're right, it isn't my business and I'm sorry Doug."

Immediately Doug began to rub the dried cum stains from the petrol tank with his shirtsleeve.

"Hey listen buddy, even if you did have a scene with him, it's none of my business. You're my partner and I have to work with you, so that's cool."

For the rest of the morning, very little was said between the two men as they went their ways in controlling the traffic.

That evening when Gary was at home with Tony, he told him of the day's happenings, which included the episode with Doug. Tony listened intently to what Gary told him, particularly the part about the come stains on the bike. Tony immediately began imagining big, butch Doug screwing some young guy over his motorbike, and he felt the tingling sensation arising between his legs as he thought about the scene. His whole face seemed to go into a trance while Gary continued to ramble on about the events of the day.

"So what's for dinner?" asked Gary, eventually.

There was no reply as Tony was still in his dream world.

"Hey little brother, wake up!"

"I'm sorry, I was just thinking about what you've been saying about Doug," replied Tony.

"And so, what's this," asked Gary grabbing the engorged bulge in the front of his brother's shorts that he was wearing and squeezing his brother's hard-on. "You've got a fucking hard-on! Where did this come from?"

Tony brushed his hand aside. "I was just imaging Doug fucking someone on his motorbike. That's quite a kinky position, if you think about it."

"And this has given you a hard-on?" he asked, again making a grab at his brother's swollen cock.

"Let go!" yelped Tony, but Gary had no intention of doing so and began horse playing with his brother. The two boys fell onto the couch in the lounge with Gary landing on top of Tony and trying to pull his shorts off. Tony tickled his older brother in an effort to throw him off, but without avail. Gary gave a huge yank at Tony's shorts and they slid down to his knees, revealing his long, hard, cock with it's beautifully shaped clipped head and a small drop of pre-come emanating from its glistening tip. Gary's mouth dived down onto its tip and licked the pre-come off. Suddenly Tony lay still as he felt his brother's warm mouth sink to the base of his cock in one swift movement.

"Mmm!" groaned Gary as his mouth rose again to the tip, where he kissed it and said, "That tastes good. Do you like the feeling?"

Tony wasn't sure how to respond to his brother, as nothing like this had ever happened before, and neither had ever spoken about male-to-male sex, let alone done anything like this with each other. Tony let a hand slide down to Gary's crotch where he felt the beginnings of something new in their relationship. When his hand gripped around Gary's ever increasing manhood, Gary looked up at Tony and smiled with a mouthful of beautiful cock.

Tony managed to release Gary's straining dick from the confines of his bike gear and gave it a gentle squeeze. He then slid his hand down its length, feeling it grow in size as he did so. Gary continued to massage Tony's dick with his mouth. They were both extremely gentle with each other, and both continued their actions as though it was part of their normal everyday lives, until Tony thrust upwards to meet Gary's mouth and said, "If you continue like this, I'm going to shoot in your mouth."

Gary removed his mouth, smiled and added, "Go for it little brother, I want to taste you," and immediately went back to working on his length.

Tony increased his upward thrusts into Gary's throat until he reached the edge of no return and with a cry, shot his first load into the depths of Gary's throat. Gary swallowed as fast as he could as the second and third shots were fired from the throbbing cannon between Tony's legs. When Tony had nothing more to give, he lay there exhausted while Gary continued to suck his brother's love juice, and then lifting his head once more, he smiled into his brother's eyes and could only exclaim, "Wow!"

"You're right about 'Wow!' that was incredible," sighed Tony, "but now it's your turn to enjoy."

Tony slid from underneath Gary and let Gary lie on his back on the couch while Tony undid his trousers and pulled them off. He licked his way up Gary's legs, pausing slightly when he reached his balls, then he gently took one then the other into his mouth and licked over their surface. Once he had saturated them, he moved to the base of Gary's 8 inch, cut dick and ran his tongue up to the tip and then around the head. He opened his mouth and slowly, applying gentle pressure, sank his mouth over Gary's cock until his chin rested against Gary's balls. He held this position and maneuvered his tongue around its girth, causing Gary to thrust deeply into his throat, almost causing him to gag, but he held himself steady and then started the journey upwards again.

Tony alternated between sucking his brother's stiff dick and licking his balls, which was gradually driving Gary towards and orgasm.

"Suck my dick!" exclaimed Gary as he neared his moment of ecstasy.

Tony obliged willingly and increased the speed with which he was doing it. Gary also increased his upward thrusts, fucking Tony's face. As Gary's cock erupted, Tony's mouth slipped from it and the first shot landed on Tony's face, but he was very quick to get that cock back down his throat and managed to take whatever Gary offered him. He sucked hard and licked Gary's cock as it throbbed in his mouth. Both boys were breathing heavily from the excitement, but even after Gary was fulfilled, Tony never took his mouth off. As Gary's began to subside and go limp, so Tony continued to work on it, making passionate love to it until both he and Gary could feel it getting hard again.

"I don't believe this," said Gary, watching his little brother work on him like a hardened expert. "You're a bloody sex maniac. Haven't you had enough?"

Tony lifted his head and laughed out loud. "Not when you've got something good in your mouth," he replied.

Gary pushed Tony away and sat up.

"Let's keep something for another time."

"You mean there'll be another time?"

"With you sucking so good like that, I'm sure that there'll be plenty of times with you," replied Gary.

The two of them sat there smiling at each other like two lovers, just thinking about what had happened between them, when Gary suddenly said, "I think Doug's into male sex, you know."

"What gives you that idea?"

"Today he had dried cum on the tank of his bike and he said that he'd had sex last night, then this young guy that we'd stopped for speeding drove up and thanked him for last night. I wonder if he had sex with the guy?"

"Maybe he's in the closet and doesn't want anyone to know," said Tony. "Maybe we should invite him around again and try him out to see if he's available."

"Actually that's not a bad idea. Hell it would be funny if he were into guys. By the way, what happened between us now, do you do that with other guys and if not, why did you do it with me?" asked Gary.

"Sure," answered Tony, "I'm gay and I like guys, but what about you? Why did you let me do it with you?"

"I've never actually done it with another guy before, but inside I know I have these feelings for some guys, but don't get me wrong I still like my women."

"When you say some guys, what sort of guys are you talking about?" asked Tony.

"I'm not into young guys, like eighteen or nineteen year olds, that sort of thing, but I rather fancy the kind like Doug; you know manly looking."

"So where do I fit in?" questioned Tony.

"Hey you're my brother and no matter what you're like, I love you and, believe it or not, I actually think you're quite sexy."

"Well thanks for the compliment, but tell me do you think Mike might be gay?"

"Who knows? Maybe he and Doug have had a thing and that's why they get on so well," laughed Gary, getting up from the couch and heading for the kitchen. "Come on, let's sort out some dinner for ourselves and make plans about those other two guys."

———————

Weeks went by and the relationships between Doug and Gary, and that of Mike and Tony developed more strongly, but Doug still never let on anything to Gary regarding the young man that they had stopped. Doug continued to see Marc occasionally, but made sure that if they had sex on the motorbike, which Marc enjoyed, there was no telltale evidence left behind that Gary might question him about.

It was nearing Christmas and the two brothers had now almost completed a year in the bike section, but they were still with their allocated partners. Gary and Tony decided to invite Doug and Mike to a party at their home, but to add spice to the evening, they told them it was going to be a theme party, but they still had to decide on the theme. During the weeks leading up to Christmas, Tony suggested a number of different themes, which Gary dismissed.

One evening, Gary said, "Seeing that we're in the bike section of the force, why don't we have a leather theme? It'll be easy for us to get outfits if we do."

Tony didn't think it a good idea as they spent every day of their working lives in leather of some sort.

"We could rig up a sling in the lounge and maybe a rack," suggested Gary.

Tony roared with laughter. "You're getting quite kinky by the sounds of things."

"I'm just trying to liven up the party for us."

After much discussion, the two brothers decided on a theme: Gladiators, masters and slaves. The idea was something Roman or even science fiction, but they were leaving it to the guests' imaginations. They produced an invitation and sent them off to Doug and Mike and in the invitation it stated that they could bring a partner if they wished.

Once the invitees had received their invitations, they said nothing about the theme. They never questioned it nor did they refuse the invitations.

The day of the party arrived and Tony and Gary spent the best part of it decorating the lounge and stocking up on food and drinks. They had made Roman standards and a few Roman helmets and shields. Gary had constructed a sling on one side of the lounge by hanging it on chains from a wooden frame, and they had scattered huge cushions around the lounge floor. Neither Gary nor Tony had discussed with each other what they were going to wear, so it would be a surprise for both of them.

As the evening neared, the food was laid out and both boys went in to their separate bedrooms to get dressed. Tony was the first to be ready and emerged from his room wearing a short type of Roman skirt, which only just covered the brief G-string of brown leather that he wore under it. How he managed to get his enormous package into that brief G-string was a miracle, but the bulge in the front was a sight to be desired. As for his upper body, he had smeared a thin coating of baby oil over his chest and arms so that they glistened in the light. He wore flat sandals on his feet with leather thongs wrapping up his legs to just below his knees.

Gary eventually came out of his room and found Tony in the kitchen.

"Wow!" exclaimed Tony when he saw Gary. "That's some outfit!"

"Hey, yours isn't too bad either," replied Gary admiring his brother's torso.

Gary had on a black leather, studded pouch, which jutted out in front of him and a pair of knee length boots. Around his neck was a studded collar and around each bicep was a leather thong. Attached to each nipple was a nipple clamp and connecting the two was a metal chain.

"Now what are you supposed to be?" asked Tony walking around Gary and admiring both the front and the back view.

"I'm a gladiator," said Gary, strutting around the kitchen, "and what about you?

"I'm going as a young man in a Roman Emperor's house."

After having passed a few compliments about each one's outfits, they busied themselves with the finishing touches to their party.

The doorbell rang and Tony went to open the door. Mike was there, standing on the doorstep dressed as a Roman legionnaire.

"Hi Mike, you look incredibly smart for a legionnaire. I'd be careful if I were you because you might get called to join the Roman army looking like that."

"I take it that's meant as a compliment?"

"Absolutely. Hey, don't stand out there, come in out of the cold."

Mike entered the warm homely atmosphere and was startled to see the way that Gary was dressed. At first his mouth dropped open and then he burst out laughing.

"What's so funny?" asked Gary, a little surprised.

"I'm sorry," replied Mike, "It's not that it's funny, it's just that I didn't expect to see you dressed like that, but you look good in it, the little that there is."

They ushered Mike into the lounge and offered him a drink. They sat talking for a while, before the doorbell rang again. This time it was Doug, but unlike Mike, who had come alone, Doug had brought a partner, in the shape of Marc. Tony opened the door for them and ushered them into the lounge.

"Hi guys," chirped Doug, "I want you to meet Marc. I hope you don't mind but it said on the invitation that I could bring a partner."

"Not at all," said Gary, a little surprised to see Marc. "Weren't you the guy we stopped for speeding?"

"That's right," answered Marc, a little timidly.

"Are you the guy with the yellow BMW?" asked Tony.

"Yes."

As the conversations continued, Tony looked at Doug and Marc together and the way they were dressed. Doug had on a leather pouch similar to the one Gary had on, but he was also wearing leather chaps and boots, while Marc had on a white tunic with a white G-string under it.

"What are you two going as?" asked Gary.

"I'm the master of the Gladiators and this is my servant," replied Doug, taking Marc by the arm and pulling him closer towards himself. "By the way, what's that thing doing in the lounge?" asked Doug pointing at the sling.

"It's just part of the décor for the Roman setting," said Gary going over to it and sitting in it. "You see it's fairly sturdy, so if you want to try it out, be my guest. Can I get drinks for you guys?"

"Thanks, two beers," replied Doug.

Marc made himself comfortable on one of the cushions while Doug and Gary went into the kitchen to get the beers from the fridge.

"Doug, I hope you don't mind me asking, but where does Marc fit in?" asked Gary as he opened the beers.

"Listen Gary, it's just that I took a fancy to him that day we stopped him."

"Are you gay then?"

"Yeah, I dig guys. Is that a problem with you?"

Gary laughed, "not at all, you go for it."

The two returned to the lounge, chatting and laughing with each other.

"What's the joke?" asked Tony as they entered the lounge.

"No joke at all," replied Gary, "Doug and I were just chatting in the kitchen, that's all."

Gary and Tony had made a buffet style dinner for their guests, which everyone thoroughly enjoyed. As they devoured the food and enjoyed their drinks, so their possible inhibitions began to disappear and they all relaxed a great deal more. Marc and Doug were lying on the cushions next to each other, and every now and then, their hands would wander onto the other's body, flicking an odd nipple or rubbing a leg against the others'. Nobody seemed to mind and soon Tony had sidled up to Mike and draped a leg over Mike's. Mike didn't seem to object, nor did he seem embarrassed by Marc and Doug's behavior, in fact he seemed to be enjoying watching them. Gary, at this stage seemed to be the odd one out, but he watched closely the antics of the other four.

Although there had been music playing all the time, Gary got up and put on a new CD. The tempo changed to something more upbeat and Marc immediately sprang to his feet and started dancing by himself. Soon Doug joined him while Tony moved some of the furniture out of the way to make more room and the two of them went into their own little world.

"Do you want to dance?" asked Tony, standing and holding out a hand to Mike as if to help him up.

"Yeah, why not," he answered, stretching out his hand and taking Tony's. Tony pulled him to his feet and the two of them joined Marc and Doug on the dance floor. Gary sat smiling as they all enjoyed themselves.

"Hey!" shouted Doug, above the music, "are going to sit there all night or are you coming to join us dance?"

"I don't know whether you have realized it but there are no more partners available," replied Gary.

"Get off your ass and come and join Marc and I; I'm sure he doesn't mind sharing, do you?"

"Not at all," came the reply.

Gary rose to his feet and was soon dancing with Marc and Doug and thoroughly enjoying himself. While the three of them were dancing together, Doug moved behind Gary and, placing his hands on Gary's hips, he held on and pressed his body against Gary's, maintaining the same movement and rhythm that Gary was using.

"Hey we make quite a good couple," remarked Doug as he pressed his crotch up against Gary's ass.

Gary didn't try to resist and kept up with the rhythm of the music. Then Marc moved closer to face Gary and put his arms around both Gary and Doug, so that his crotch was pressed hard against Gary's. Again Gary did try to resist. All three were 'attached' to each other, swaying in time to the music, while Mike and Tony had now come into closer contact.

As they danced, Gary could feel the start of a hard-on forming in his studded pouch, and was well aware that soon Marc would feel it too. As his dick grew in size, so Marc tended to gyrate more forcefully against Gary's crotch, while at the same time he was convinced he felt Doug's hard cock prodding against his asshole. As the music came to an end, Gary broke away from the other two and went to put on another CD. While he did so, Marc and Doug stood with their arms around each other's neck, whispering in each other's ear. As the music started up again, Doug led Marc to the sling, where he began to disrobe him. Gary, in the meantime had gone back into the kitchen to fetch a couple more beers for the boys, while Mike and Tony watched bemused at what Doug was doing to Marc. By the time that Gary returned, Marc had been stripped naked and was placed in the sling on his back with his legs dangling over the side. His long cock stood erect and Doug stroked it very gently while Marc lay there groaning with pleasure. Tony and Mike watched in awe as Doug bent over and swallowed Marc's enormous cock right down to its base and held that position for a while before resurfacing to its tip. Tony began rubbing his own swelling cock and disentangled his Roman skirt that he was wearing. It dropped to the floor, leaving him only in his brown leather G-string, which was straining to hide his very hard and erect cock. His hands continued to slide up and down the length of his covered cock as he watched Doug work on Marc's hard-on.

Both Gary and Mike watched Tony move closer to the sling and stand on the side adjacent to Marc. Marc smiled at Tony and stretched out a hand to cup Tony's balls. Once Marc had hold of them, he pulled Tony closer to his side, and, using both hands, proceeded to relieve Tony's cock of its pressure. He pulled the G-string down so that Tony's beautiful cock sprang to life. Marc once again took hold of Tony's cock and pulled it towards his mouth where he engulfed it with his hot mouth. He slurped along its length, while Doug did likewise to him.

Mike felt that he wanted to be part of the action so he moved to the other side of Marc and faced Tony. Tony stretched across Marc's body and ran his fingers over Mike's nipples until he felt them harden, and then he squeezed them gently. He undid Mike's Centurion's toga and let it fall to the ground, leaving Mike standing in a Speedo costume, which he had on underneath. Marc removed his mouth from Tony's cock and moved his head towards Mike's, letting his wet lips run along the material covered bulge. Doug stood up and lifted Marc's legs until they latched into the leather straps attached to the sling, and then proceeded to work on Marc's balls and the area between the base of his ball and his asshole.

Watching all this action taking place was too much for Gary, because very soon he had his cock in his hand and was salivating over it to lubricate it more for easier friction. He moved in behind Doug and ran both hands over Doug's well-rounded, yet firm ass. Doug groaned and thrust his ass back towards Gary, who squeezed both cheeks and smacked them fairly firmly. Doug's cock throbbed as Gary did this and he once again thrust back. However, Gary was busy removing his leather pouch so that his cock was free to search like a periscope in the air. Doug's leather pouch had a clasp to it, which Gary undid allowing the pouch to drop to the ground, leaving Doug only in his chaps and boots. Gary let his cock rub up against the crack of Doug's ass, letting him feel the length and warmth of his cock. Each time that Gary did this, Doug pushed back so that his ass was tight against Gary's cock.

In the meantime, Mike had moved around the sling to the same side as Tony and had positioned himself in the same way as Gary, but behind Tony. Marc continued to suck on Tony's length while Mike grabbed a condom and some lube that was conveniently placed nearby. He opened the pack and unrolled the condom over the full length of his uncut dick, pulling his foreskin as far back as it would go as he did so. He then smeared some of the lube on his swollen cock and slowly began the penetrating journey into Tony. Tony froze for a moment to become accustomed to Mike's size and then gave in, allowing Mike full entry. Gary had also equipped himself with his condom and had also placed one on Doug's cock. As Doug aimed for Marc's asshole, so Gary aimed for Doug's, and the two men made their entries simultaneously.

All five men were gasping and moaning as they indulged in their wildest fantasies.

As Gary ploughed into Doug, so he gripped the hunk's large nipples and twisted them, creating a pain, which to Doug was more like pleasure than pain. Doug became wild with excitement the more Gary fucked and pinched him and as a result, Marc's ass took a battering, much to his pleasure. At the same time, Tony was experiencing the gentle, deep thrusts from Mike, who was nearing the point of no return.

"I'm getting close," groaned Mike.

"Fuck me hard, then," shouted Tony, as he increased his pushing back onto Mike's cock and Marc fought to take hold of Tony's cock with his mouth.

"Aagh! I'm coming," shouted Mike and Tony felt the warm shots entering the condom as it filled within his inside. When Mike had emptied his load in Tony, he gently pulled out, removed the condom and went around to the other side and started to suck on Marc's long cock in order to give him pleasure. Although Mike's mouth was plugged to Marc's cock, he still continued to wank his own cock, as though trying to get it ready for another round.

Gary looked at his little brother being given a wet treatment from Marc's full lips and nodded his head as if to tell Tony to take his place. Tony pulled away from Marc and picked up a condom, which he placed on his hard, wet dick and moved to where Gary was. Gary immediately pulled out of Doug, who gave a disappointed groan, but was soon moaning happily again when he felt a cock back inside of him, but this time it was Tony's full length. Tony ploughed his cock into Doug with renewed vigor, causing the sling to swing backwards and forwards. Gary positioned himself behind his brother and, unlike with Doug, he gently and with feeling entered his brother. Tony felt a warm glowing feeling as Gary's cock slid slowly into his depths, without there being any pain.

The feeling for Gary was immense as Tony's ass felt tighter than Doug's and this created an intense feeling in Gary's groins. So intense was the feeling that he knew that he too was about to shoot his load.

"Oh God, this feels so good; I'm going to shoot!" exclaimed Gary, as he pounded harder into Tony and lost all gentleness. Tony responded by thrusting back onto Gary, trying to keep the whole of Gary's 8 inches inside of him, and as he did so, Doug did likewise as he didn't want to lose Tony's cock inside of him. With the sudden, deep thrust from Gary as he fired into Tony, so Tony pounded into Doug who let fly and started shooting into Marc. Both Gary and Doug were groaning in pleasure as they both erupted into the men in their lives. When Doug was complete, his sweat-covered body slumped forward across Marc and he took over from Mike and sucked hard on Marc's cock in an effort to get him to shoot. In doing so, Tony sank deeper into Doug's ass and this brought on an ecstatic feeling and his body shivered as he shot into Doug's ass.

"Aaagh fuck!" shouted Tony. "Oh yeah, oh fuck," and he kept pounding and shooting while his big brother ran his huge hands over Tony's smooth butt, fingering his hole.

When all five boys had exhausted themselves, they collapsed on the cushions laughing and glowing.

"I didn't know you were into this sort of thing, Gary!" said Doug, breathing heavily from his tiring episode.

"I'm not really, but seeing you going at it was a turn-on and I just had to have that ass of yours, but then halfway through, I also wanted to have Tony's, so I had the best of both worlds and I thoroughly enjoyed it; but what about you?"

"What do you mean?" asked Doug.

"I had my suspicions about you, but I wasn't sure; and what about Mike?"

"I've always been this way, even though I did try marriage once, but it was actually Doug who confirmed things for me," replied Mike.

"Yeah, you see when I joined the force, the first person I was teamed up with was Mike and we got on very well."

"So well in fact," interrupted Mike, "that we had a scene together which lasted for some time, but Doug seems more into younger guys. Any rate we're still the best of mates, aren't we?"

"Sure are," continued Doug, "in fact whenever I need a bit of sex and I can't pick any up, I go round to Mike's and he satisfies me, don't you buddy?"

"Sure do!"

"But what about you Gary?" asked Mike.

"I still like my women, but there's no getting away from a nice tight-assed guy who can milk my cock for me, and I now know that both Tony and Doug can do it, so some time I'm going to have to try Mike and Marc."

From that day on, Gary and Tony's relationship as brothers became much closer and many an evening was spent in the company of either Mike or Doug. Of course, in time Doug dropped Marc, but they still remained friends.

- ABOUT THE AUTHOR -

Lew Bull, who lives in Johannesburg, South Africa, has been published in a number of anthologies including, among others, *Ultimate Gay Erotica 2007* and *2008; Travelrotica for Gay Men* and *Travelrotica vol.2; Fast Balls; Dorm Porn 2; Treasure Trail; My First Time vol.5; Secret Slaves* and *Ultimate Undies.* Recently he was also published in *Cruise Lines; Don't Ask, Don't Tie Me Up-Military BDSM Fantasies; Taken by Force; Boys Will Be Boys; Special Forces* and *Sextime: Erotic Stories of Time Travel.*

Although he is involved in education, and has a Doctorate in this field, it is writing and travelling that brings him most pleasure.

Lew Bull is also the author of the novels **Power Buddies; Wet, Wild and Willing; The Bonds of Friendship** and **Caribbean Cruising**. Available at your local bookstore, Amazon.com or The NazcaPlainsCorp.com.

POWER BUDDIES

Power
Buddies

a novel by
LEW BULL

A BONER BOOK

Bull

Caribbean Cruising

Caribbean Cruising

a novel by
Lew Bull

A
Boner
Book

Bull

The Bonds of Friendship

The Bonds of Friendship

a novel by

Lew Bull

A Botier Book

www.ingramcontent.com/pod-product-compliance
Lightning Source LLC
Chambersburg PA
CBHW051119260626
47170CB00005B/1580